HASMON

Hasmonean Primary
School

This book has been donated by

Natalie Corin &
Lisa Benisti

Choices

Choices

A Novel

by
Miriam L. Elias

FIRST EDITION
First Impression . . . March 1996

Published by
TAMAR BOOKS

Distributed by
MESORAH PUBLICATIONS, Ltd.
4401 Second Avenue
Brooklyn, New York 11232
(718) 921-9000

Distributed in Europe by
J. LEHMANN HEBREW BOOKSELLERS
20 Cambridge Terrace
Gateshead, Tyne and Wear
England NE8 1RP

Distributed in Israel by
SIFRIATI / A. GITLER—BOOKS
4 Bilu Street
P.O.B. 14075
Tel Aviv 61140

Distributed in Australia & New Zealand by
GOLDS BOOK & GIFT CO.
36 William Street
Balaclava 3183, Vic., Australia

Distributed in South Africa by
KOLLEL BOOKSHOP
22 Muller Street
Yeoville 2198, Johannesburg, South Africa

Printed in the United States of America by Noble Book Press Corp.
Bound by Sefercraft, Quality Bookbinders, Ltd. Brooklyn, N.Y.

This book is dedicated
to the memory of
Mrs. Buna Shulman, ע″ה
a true Eishes Chayil,
an outstanding Mechaneches,
and a greatly valued, very dear friend.

M.L.E.

My sincerest thanks to:
Mrs. Rivkah Kreitman
Mrs. Rivky Marcus
and Miss Chana Liba Klein

for their kind, unstinting help, cheerfully given,
on various aspects of this book.

ראה אנכי נתן לפניכם היום ברכה וקללה.
את הברכה אשר תשמעו אל מצות ה׳ אלקיכם
אשר אנכי מצוה אתכם היום.

See, I present before you today
a blessing and a curse.
The blessing: that you hearken
to the commandments of Hashem, your G-d,
that I command you today.

(Devarim 11:26-27)

החיים והמות נתתי לפניך, הברכה והקללה,
ובחרת בחיים . . .

I have placed life and death before you,
blessing and curse;
and you shall choose life . . .

(Devarim 30:19)

Part One

Chapter One

The room looked like a bargain bazaar at the end of a busy day. Sara Citron stood ankle deep in discarded clothing, staring at herself in the full-length mirror. She had finally decided on her dark-blue Bis skirt, with a blue-and-white top. Her face was flushed, and despite the air conditioning, she was perspiring profusely from all the changing of clothes and the excitement that filled her so completely; she thought she'd burst.

Now she began working on her hair; side part and loose, or half-pony with the new leather barrette? Her glasses fogged up again so she could only see herself, and the bed behind her piled high with odds and ends, in a pearly mist. What would Mrs. Deutch consider the proper look for an at-home conference such as this?

The phone rang and she reached for the receiver while her eyes darted madly about the room, searching for her sneakers.

"Hello?"

"Hi! Is she there yet?"

"Any minute, and I'm nowhere near ready. Natalie, I'm going out of my mind! I'll have to hang up on you. I think I'm going to change again. I'm wearing that blue-and-white striped top with the gold buttons on the shoulder. All wrong, right?"

"Sounds great! Wear the gold scrunchy and RELAX! And Sara, call me the minute she leaves!" There went her last link with normal life as she'd known it.

Sara gave her thick, blonde hair another vigorous brushing and twisted the gold scrunchy into place. She'd never find her sneakers unless she took the time to wipe her glasses! They had to be here somewhere. She dove under the bed, reaching out as far as she could. Bingo! Found one — one to go.

She straightened up and stumbled over the second sneaker, which had been hiding under a pile of 'rejects.'

"Sara? You all right?" Mom's voice floated down the hall.

"Coming!" Sara sounded cool, but she was sure that Mom wasn't fooled. If anyone understood what all this was about, it was her mother.

Mom had baked three kinds of cookies, and the fridge was packed with a variety of drinks. Although the Citrons were strictly kosher, just to be on the safe side (you never knew with *kollel* people like the Deutches) Sara had also arranged a platter with beautiful fresh fruit and carefully sealed it with plastic wrap. It sat in sparkling splendor on the lowest shelf.

Daddy wasn't home, of course; it was the middle of the day. But basically and reluctantly, he had already given his consent.

Sara wrestled frantically with the knots in the laces of her Keds. She was clumsy, and furious with herself. Did everything have to go wrong?

The bell rang. Mom would have to let her in. Sara bit her lip to hold back the tears. She'd practiced countless times in front of the mirror exactly how she would look when she opened the door for her teacher, and had settled on a semi-smile to fit the seriousness of the occasion. Oh, well, so much for that!

She heard their voices moving from the front door, through the kitchen, and out to the patio.

One final check in the mirror; no more procrastinating! With her heart in her throat, she tiptoed down the hall and stepped up to the bay window in the kitchen, By carefully lifting one of the slats in the miniblinds, she could clearly observe the two outside.

Mom, wearing her denim skirt and matching snood, seemed full of good cheer and smiles. Sara could hardly contain all the love she felt for her mother right then. If I ever really do leave, she thought, I'll get ill from homesickness, that's for sure!

Mrs. Deutch was perfect, as usual. She wore her tan skirt and vest, with a white embroidered blouse. Her *sheitel* looked like combed silk — long, straight, dark blonde, and shiny. She sat turned toward Mrs. Citron, focused entirely on what was being said. Occasionally her eyes stared off into the distance as if she were groping for whatever she wanted to answer.

Did she notice the picnic table that Mr. Citron shored up every few months by nailing odd pieces of wood to the splintering base? What did she think of their beaten-up glider and beach chairs? Or the garden hose, from which water trickled silently and sadly across the patio because the faucet needed a new washer? And the grass, strewn gaily with thousands of dandelions and assorted cousins?

It was hard to tell. It certainly seemed as if she saw none of these and was totally caught up in the conversation.

Sara licked her lips and realized she was parched. Then, with a silent prayer, she grabbed the fruit and some plates and stepped outside. With a mumbled "Hi" in the general direction of Mrs. Deutch, she set things on the umbrella table and immediately fled back to safety in the kitchen. She knew she was flushed and flustered, and found herself hissing out loud, "Stop acting like a 9-year-old, for goodness' sake!" Then, armed with the cookies and drinks, she stepped outside again and sat on the edge of the picnic bench. They were just discussing Daddy's feelings on the subject. Yes, he had now given his permission for her to go, but the decision had clearly been made to please his wife and daughter. He was convinced that what was good enough for 12-year-old Danny was also fine for 15-year-old Sara. And besides, the community here in Dalton, Texas was making such enormous strides, Jewishly speaking, that running to Montford, a suburb of New York, really seemed to be going a bit too far!

"I'm just as pleased as he is with all the good things that are happening here," said Sara's mother. "But I can understand Sara's wanting even more. I'm very excited for her and *with* her, if you see what I mean, Mrs. Deutch. You've opened her eyes to what's out there, and I say good for her if she has the desire and ambition to go all out for it. At her age I think I'd have been exactly the same."

"Yes, I agree that we should help Sara achieve what she wants so much. I must say it's wonderful that Mr. Citron's on our side now, and of course that makes it all so much nicer." Mrs. Deutch looked straight at Sara when she said this. She knew how Sara had agonized over her father's objections, sometimes even to the point of giving up.

"Now tell us about the logistics." said Mrs. Citron. "I know that Montford's about an hour from New York. We have relatives in Queens, but I realize that that's not practical as far as boarding is concerned. She'd have to be placed in Montford, right?"

Mrs. Deutch beamed a smile straight at Sara.

"No problem! We've always had girls from faraway places studying at the Bais Yaakov, and there are invariably families who want to have a boarder. I will get busy myself, *b'li neder,* and make sure to find the best possible home for Sara."

"How will I be able to fit into their 10th grade when they've had all this intensive Hebrew learning for so many years?" Sara found herself putting her secret fears into words.

"I'm sure you'll be needing some extra tutoring, but they're equipped to provide that, and we all know you're not exactly slow," Mrs. Deutch said, winking at Mom. "She'll be up there with the best of them in no time. And as for English, you might even find yourself ahead, Sara!" Again she stared into the distance, and then said thoughtfully, "Personally, I think there's probably a great deal those girls can learn from *you!*"

Sara felt herself blush. No teacher, however long she'd been in school, would ever be able to hold a candle to Mrs. Deutch! Beautiful, inside and out. That's what she was.

There were many more details to discuss, and while Mom passed the refreshments, Sara felt herself relaxing and actually enjoying herself. Mom explained that they would need a partial scholarship, and that Sara would have to find some kind of work in the evenings to earn her pocket money. The problem of board and lodging costs remained. Mrs. Deutch remembered that sometimes there were families who, in exchange for some help with younger children or household tasks, took girls in free of charge. She'd let them know.

Sara knew it wasn't going to be easy. Natalie thought she was altogether crazy for going and had tried in vain to talk Sara out of it. But there was this drive deep inside her, and she was determined to give it her best effort.

School here in Dalton had already begun. In Montford they only started after Labor Day, so there was plenty of time to get ready. The gap between herself and her friends would widen even before she left.

Hours later, Sara settled back on her pillow and switched off the reading light. A gentle breeze from the open window fanned her face and wafted about the small room like a dancing veil. She squeezed her eyes tightly shut and lay perfectly still, breathing deeply.

Thinking time! Press the 'play button.' Start! Scene One! —

She was back in her room at two in the afternoon, trying to decide what to wear. On the dark screen of her mind's eye, Sara recaptured the entire sequence of events.

Here she was, studying herself in the mirror, while talking to Natalie. What would life in Montford be without Natalie? Sometimes, at the oddest moments, in the middle of class or when she was brushing her teeth or walking through the mall right next to her friend, with her thick, black braid lying over her shoulder, she would mutter under her breath: 'Thank You, G-d, for Natalie. Thanks loads!'

Maybe Natalie was the way she was because her father was Dr. Sarnoff, and there was so much human suffering, major and minor, coming and going through that house that the care-giving instinct rubbed off on all of them. It wasn't as if Dr. Sarnoff worked in a medical building or a hospital. His office was right downstairs in their house, with a separate entrance, so that patients and family were under one roof, and the roles of doctor and father interchanged a hundred times a day. But whatever it was, Sara thought, those parents and kids had hearts as big as hay barns, and love and compassion enough to overflow and share with everyone.

This whole adventure would have been twice as exciting if Natalie had come along, and much less scary! But Natalie was proud of being a Daltonite. She felt like a pioneer in building up *Yiddishkiet* here in Texas, and in a strange way, her long-distance view of Jewish life in New York wasn't the least attractive or desirable.

"I bet they're a bunch of spoiled brats," she'd say. "And millions of them, too. Over here we're few, but first quality! I know I sound like a snob. Can't help it."

All this was truly how Natalie felt, but Sara knew that below the surface there were more factors in the equation. Natalie had never gone off to sleep-away camp; she was the kind who got homesick at a slumber party, though she'd never admit it. Natalie needed her nest, and Sara had come to terms with the idea of going away by herself.

Scene Two: The Patio Scene!

Sara saw herself perched on the very edge of the picnic bench, chewing her nails and trying to absorb the unbelievable fact that here was a real decision in the making. At last!

No! This needed more than her usual night game of video recall. Sara threw back her cover and padded across the worn, shaggy carpet to the window. If she leaned way over the sill and turned her head to the left, she could see exactly where they'd been sitting a few hours ago. She smiled and stared, fascinated.

'That's me,' she thought. 'I need to lock scenes like this into a frame that I can carry in my memory box, to relive and to remember. How many passengers had their faces pressed to the window to get that last glimpse of *Eretz Yisrael* when the plane lifted off from Lud last summer? She had! Were there others who gave the *chupah* a second glance after *chasan* and *kallah* had walked back up the aisle? She did! And each year, when it came time to say good-bye to the *succah* with the special *Y'he Ratzon,* she'd stand and take time out to delight in it all and to savor the special aura of Succos one last time.

The patio, awash with silver light from a perfectly round, full moon, was just such a scene. Beautiful, luminous, silent, all the shabby imperfections now invisible, it had taken on the glamour of magic. Here, this afternoon, in bright daylight, the decision had been made. It was final. Sara would move to Montford for 10th grade.

Chapter Two

Al Citron and his wife Lisa picked Sara up at Newark Airport. Al was Daddy's cousin, and although half a continent divided them, they had always kept up a family relationship, sharing news and views via the occasional telephone call and Rosh Hashanah mail. Al had been delighted to help out, stipulating only that they should try to book a Sunday flight so that both he and Lisa would be free from work and could take time out to drive Sara all the way to Montford.

"How are we going to know her?" he'd asked. "Will she wear a Dallas Cowboy football shirt?"

"Not our Sara," Daddy had answered, laughing out loud. "I have a better idea; I'll send you a picture. But truthfully, I think you'd recognize her anyway; she's a Citron, all right." And the date had been set.

"Perfect match!" said Lisa, clutching the snapshot as Sara walked over to them at the terminal gate. "Welcome to the Big Apple!"

Sara couldn't believe her eyes. They had told her that Al was tall and looked like an older version of Daddy, and that Lisa, by contrast, appeared even shorter than she really was. But Sara found herself actually looking down into the merry, smiling eyes of this dark-haired, diminutive, newly found cousin.

They whisked her down to baggage claim and divided their attention between scanning the moving conveyer belt for Sara's luggage and getting acquainted.

"Do you mind if I call you Uncle Al and Aunt Lisa?" Sara blurted out. "It would be so much easier. I asked Mom, and she said she was sure you wouldn't mind."

"Go right ahead," said Al. Turning to his wife, he added, with a chuckle, "That'll really make us feel like responsible adults."

Sara bit her lip. She should have let it go.

"Don't worry about it, Sara. I was only joking. Sure — you call us whatever makes you comfortable. Right, honey?"

"Of course. And I understand exactly how you feel," said Lisa, laying her hand lightly on Sara's arm.

Twenty minutes later, after storing her belongings safely in the trunk of the Buick, they were on their way. Sara watched the passing scenery while answering a barrage of questions. How were Mom and Dad and little Danny?

"Not so little any more. He's just turned 12," she said, and would have liked to add, 'Old enough to be a royal pain in the neck sometimes,' but the recent separation was already working its magic, tinting everything left behind in a rosy glow.

"Now, this family Rudin you're going to be staying with," said Al over his shoulder as he maneuvered his car through the streaming traffic on the New Jersey Turnpike, "something about the name rings a bell. Does it sound familiar to you, Lisa?"

"Rudin — Rudin —" Lisa, forehead creased, gave the matter her entire attention.

Sara's stomach was beginning to act up.

Pure nerves, she told herself. But it had better not get much worse. She tried to push visions of herself throwing up all over this plush car into the back of her mind.

"Do you mind if I open the window a crack?" she asked.

"Sure, go ahead," said Lisa. "Don't you feel well, dear?"

"I'm okay." Sara managed a wan smile. "Just need a little fresh air."

"What does he do, this Rudin?" Al persisted.

"Something in real estate, I think," said Sara. "And his wife's home full time. They have a number of kids, and the oldest girl is a senior in the school I'll be attending."

Her stomach lurched and bobbed about like a well-done matzoh ball in a pot of bubbling chicken soup. She rested her head against the soft upholstery and closed her eyes, hoping to give the impression of having dozed off.

Good! She felt just a little better and took a peek. Lisa, finger on lips and motioning to the back seat, said, "Shhh!" and Al drove on in silence.

Sara swallowed hard. Her mind flew back home over the hills, fields, and waterways she had just traversed. Mom and Daddy had probably made an outdoor barbecue tonight. Some of Danny's friends would have joined them for supper and might now be throwing a ball lazily back and forth. She could almost hear the thwack of the ball as it pounded into the catcher's mitt, the scent of charcoal still lingering in the evening air.

Did she wish she were there? No, not really; not if she was honest. Right now, dizzy with nervous tension, worried about how she would look to her new family, and not yet at ease even with Al and Lisa, she nevertheless had to admit that here is where she wanted to be at this moment.

They'd arrive at about 9 o'clock, she figured. Just early enough to get to know everyone, and late enough to be able to flee to bed before the newness became too hard to handle.

"Hey! Meyer Rudin — of course! The *shaatnez* guy! He was from Montford. Remember?" Lisa appealed to Al.

"Oh, yes! That's it!" said Al, slapping his knee with the left hand and steering expertly with the other.

"Thanks, honey. You're a true genius. This was really getting to me." Addressing Sara via the rearview mirror, he explained. "I simply can't stand not being able to place people. Like names, faces, whatever. If Lisa hadn't suddenly remembered, I would have spent sleepless hours tonight trying to match this name with a face, y'know?

"See, in our *shul,* they organize a Sunday brunch once a month, and they bring in speakers on different topics having to do with *ha-lachah* — very nice! One time we had *t'vilas keilim,* what to *toivel* and what not, and how to go about it. Another time a fellow spoke about an *eiruv* for carrying on Shabbos; stuff like that.

"Well, about six months ago, I guess, we had this Meyer Rudin speaking about *shaatnez.*"

"Really?" Sara was eager to hear more. "The teacher from Dalton who helped place me didn't know the family all that well."

"Oh, yes. He was really nice," said Lisa. "I mean, talking about wool and linen in coat collars is not exactly a fascinating subject. But somehow he managed to get all of us involved and interested. He's a warm, funny, friendly sort of guy, and he knows his material — excuse the pun!" She giggled.

"Lisa's right. Seems he's been doing this for years, and by now he's an outstanding authority in his field."

Al veered sharply to the left.

"Oops! I nearly missed the exit. This is it; we're almost there. I know we're on Route 26 now, and after the first light — Hmm — a right on Azure Avenue, and then — Willow Ridge Drive! This is it!" He sounded as if he'd won the New York lottery ticket for the day. "Wow! Some street! Lisa, look at these homes! Wanna move to Montford, honey?"

Slowly they drove on, staring right and left at magnificent houses, each with its own distinct architecture and landscaping.

'Oh, no!' Sara thought. 'I don't belong here. These are million-aires or something. Must be!' She gaped at the profusion of flowers under sprinklers which were turned on for the evening, coating all the colors in glistening brilliance.

Lisa sucked her breath in.

"You're a lucky girl, Sara. And I just know they'll be wonderful people. Your teacher must have made sure of that. Now, what number was it — 153, right? That must be further down on the left; here's 97 — 99 —"

"What are all these cars?" asked Al as they came to a slow crawl. "What's going on here?"

Number 153 was all lit up — two floors of it! — sprawling grey-stone, windows glittering, lights winking from behind the shrubbery along the circular drive. Cars were parked along both sides of the street for what seemed like miles and miles.

Were they in the right place? Sara pulled out the creased and crumpled scrap of paper she had kept in her skirt pocket. 'M. Rudin, 153 Willow Ridge Drive,' with the telephone number underneath.

This was it; no mistake about it.

How could they walk into this palace of a house, where some gala affair was obviously in full swing, dressed as they were?

"Uncle Al," Sara whispered. "What are we going to do?"

"Not to worry," said Al. "We'll pretend we're the kitchen help and sneak around to the back entrance. I'll be the butler."

"And I'll be the parlormaid," added Lisa, getting into the spirit of things. She wriggled out of the car and opened the trunk, lifting out the biggest suitcase. "And you, my pet, will be Cinderella, the scullery drudge," she said to Sara. "Here's your tote; now, let's get a move on."

Without any trouble, they found a paved path that led all the way around the house to the kitchen door. Peering through the glass panels, Sara observed several ladies putting finishing touches on some fruit platters as they nibbled from an array of fantastic cook-ies and petit fours.

"I wanna go home!" she hissed into Lisa's ear.

"Not on your life, you silly little goose. You'll love it here! Can't you see how I'm turning greener with envy by the minute?" She picked up her fist and, without a backward glance at Al, gave two determined raps on the door.

The ladies looked up in surprise and seemed to be calling some-one. A minute later, a girl of about 17 slipped back a bolt and cautiously opened the door. The minute she saw Sara, a bright smile lit up her face.

"Oh, hi there! You must be Sara," she cried. "Why didn't you come in the front way? And these are your cousins, right?"

'It's going to be okay,' Sara thought. 'This girl's a doll. Oh, but her heart was beating like mad. What would happen now?'

Al put the luggage in a corner of the kitchen, out of everyone's way, and wiped his forehead with a huge handkerchief.

"Hello," he began, addressing the girl. "I'm Al Citron, and this is Lisa, my wife. I had no idea you had a function here tonight. Sara could have slept over with us, and I'd have —"

"No! No way! We're so happy she's here. We're having this party tonight for a *yeshivah* with handicapped children, but we were definitely expecting her. Please sit down. Sorry everything's a bit hectic around here tonight. I'll go get my mother," said the girl. Before she dashed off she turned to add, "Oh, I *am* sorry. I forgot to introduce myself; I'm Shira Rudin. Okay, now just give me a second and we'll be right back."

One of the ladies helped Sara find some folding chairs, and armed with tall glasses of punch tinkling with ice cubes, the three newcomers gratefully sat back, exchanging smiles with those who came and went, carrying, fetching, and filling pitchers and bowls.

Moments later, an adult replica of Shira came bustling in, smiling a warm welcome.

"Good evening. I'm Faye Rudin, and you're Mr. and Mrs. Citron — and, of course, Sara. How wonderful! Now, you must come along with me. We can't hear ourselves talk here, can we? Let me help you carry these," she said, indicating the bags, and picking up Sara's carry-on, she led the way out of the kitchen and into a glass-enclosed walkway that connected to a separate wing of the house.

Sara lay stiffly between the smooth, cool sheets, her back rigid, hands clenched at her sides. It was impossible to unwind. Every nerve in her body was tense, coiled like a spring.

Uncle Al had called Texas to confirm their safe arrival, and Sara had barely managed to croak, "Hello!" Mom and Daddy had probably chalked it up to the long trip and not insisted on a lengthy description of her new home and family.

A good thing, too. She'd been quite overwhelmed at seeing this incredible mansion, and all the more so, seeing it for the first time, in lit-up splendor, smack in the middle of some kind of *tzedakah* party.

While they had made their way through the glass corridor, Mrs. Rudin had explained, "This is the Rebbetzin's wing. She sleeps in the room right next to you and the other girl."

What other girl? What did it mean? Who was the Rebbetzin? The door of the room adjoining hers had been closed. Sara looked about her. The second twin bed was neatly made up, presumably for another boarder. Thinking back, she now remembered that Mrs. Deutch had mentioned that possibly there would be two girls placed at the Rudins'. Somehow this tidbit of information had floated over her head, and she'd never given it another thought. Now, the waiting bed, the extra drawers and closet space made it all very real. Tomorrow night, it seemed, there'd be two of them in this beautiful, spacious room.

Mrs. Rudin had repeatedly offered food and something to drink before retiring, but Sara had managed to convince her that the kosher dinner on the plane had been more than enough. All she'd wanted, at that point, was to be left to herself, to absorb all these new impressions. After fussing over her for another 10 minutes, Mrs. Rudin had apologized profusely about having to abandon her so soon, explaining that she had to get back to the party. She'd added that Shira was putting on a choir for the ladies tonight, something she didn't want to miss.

Sara had assured her that she'd be fine, and had found herself, at last, in silent solitude.

So much to sort out!

What would Natalie say? "Didn't I tell you they'd be a bunch of spoiled brats? Get a load of that pile of bricks."

In the darkness, Sara smiled. Perhaps it was really a good thing that her friend had decided to opt out. She herself wasn't so quick to make judgments. Time would tell a great deal. Sounds of car doors being slammed reached her in a faraway, muffled sort of way. She was finally losing her battle with fatigue. Sara turned on her side, mumbled her *Kriyas Shema,* and willed herself to relax and meet oblivion halfway.

Chapter Three

"Can I come in?" It was a noisy stage whisper. "It's me, Shira."

Sara opened her eyes, and checked the clock on the night-stand: 9:25. Oh, no! How embarrassing! But she was wide awake, instantly alert and exited.

"Yes, come on in!" she called, sitting up and pulling her cover up around her.

Shira tiptoed inside, a finger to her lips.

"No noise! The Rebbetzin's still sleeping." 'Shira was fully dressed and must have been up for hours,' Sara thought.

"I hope you're not mad at me for getting you up now, but I just couldn't hold out another minute. I'm dying to hear all about you and your school — and I'm so sorry I never got back to you last night, but I had to do this choir and —"

"That's okay," said Sara. "I'm very glad you woke me up. I'd have slept all day. Wait for me, all right?"

She pulled on her summer robe and made her way to the bathroom across the hall.

By the time she was back, Shira had settled herself on the other twin bed and was studying the family picture Sara had set up on the dresser last night.

"Hungry?" she asked.

"No, thanks," Sara answered, sitting down in one of the two white wicker armchairs. "By the way, who's the Rebbetzin?"

Shira continued her study of the picture while she answered.

"It's my grandmother's oldest sister — we call her Tante Risha. Sounds complicated, no? Well, it's really not. My father's parents live in a small apartment on the Upper West Side in New York. They just have one bedroom. So when the Rav, Tante Risha's husband, was *niftar,* she was left all alone in Toronto. See, they never had children. First she managed there by herself, but her legs aren't that great, and we had all the extra room, so — that's the Rebbetzin."

"Hm!" said Sara. "And who's the girl that's coming today?"

"She's from Brooklyn. Her father's sick and they're going to give him treatments in the Mayo Clinic; my mother knows all the details. Anyhow, they divided up the other kids with family, but Edie didn't like that idea. So her parents arranged for her to board in Montford and go to Bais Yaakov until, *b'ezras Hashem,* her parents can come home."

Shira put the picture back and changed positions.

"I like your family. Tell me about Dalton and your school. I've never been west of New York State."

It was easy and fun to talk with this girl, who made her feel immediately at home. Sara found herself giving a vivid picture of life in Dalton, but she held back when the questions probed too deeply.

"What made you want to leave? Like, it sounds pretty interesting living out there," Shira wanted to know.

"Oh, it's hard to explain. I dunno, really. Adventure, maybe?" Sara grinned.

When Shira left her to get dressed, Sara felt she'd made a friend. She explored her room a little further, and then the luxurious bathroom with its thick, fluffy, pink towels. After a quick shower she carefully selected a skirt and blouse, brushed her hair till it did what she wanted, and neatly made up her bed.

The Rebbetzin's door was still closed, but this time Sara detected some sounds from within.

The kitchen was now an immaculate expanse of black, white, and chrome, with a bright, spacious eating area at one end, leading straight to the den. "Some breakfast nook!" Natalie would have said. "Bigger than our dining room!" No one would have guessed that only last night there had been a major social gathering here.

Hearing her come, Shira was there in a minute with her sister, 11-year-old Yocheved.

"D'you want to *daven* and take something to eat? And then we'll give you a tour of the house. Yocheved, get the juice, okay?"

Later, when Yocheved led the way, Sara thought she'd never seen two sisters so different. Shira was dark and bubbly, just like Mrs. Rudin; Yocheved was green-eyed and blonde, with very fine straight hair, and studious looking, with her glasses perched on a small straight nose. She was shy with Sara, but obviously excited to have her here and to be able to show her around.

Leading from the kitchen through a second glassed-in walkway, they showed her the second wing of the house.

"Here's where you'll be helping Uncle Meyer," said Yocheved quietly, opening the door to a workroom similar to a tailor's shop.

Sara stood stock still. UNCLE MEYER? So the *shaatnez* man wasn't her Mr. Rudin at all!

"I thought it was your father who checked for *shaatnez*," she blurted out.

The two girls burst into gales of laughter.

"My father can't tell velvet from burlap," said Shira. "That's not his speed. Besides, *shaatnez* work needs the patience of a saint, and my father's never in one place for more than a second. No; this is our uncle's '*Kodesh Kedoshim*.' He works here every evening from 7 to 10, and the two girls who helped him here last year have graduated high school and will be off to seminary soon. I guess that's where you come in."

Sara looked skeptical.

"They liked it," Yocheved said, so softly that Sara felt almost as if a comforting hand had been placed in hers.

"What's in the second room?" she asked.

They took her through the archway and showed her rows of clothing racks holding garments sheathed in plastic — those that had been checked and those that were waiting.

"Uncle Meyer is the sixth-grade *rebbi* in the Yeshivah of Montford," explained Shira. "He lives in a section called North Montford, and with his family, *kein ayin hara,* they haven't got an extra inch to spare for all of this. He's been using this wing for his *shaatnez*-testing for years! You'll meet him tonight."

She must remember to tell Uncle Al and Aunt Lisa who their Meyer Rudin really was. So here was where she would earn her spending money. She supposed Edie, the other boarder, would work with her.

"You'll get plenty of exercise just jogging around this place." said Shira, indicating the grounds through the glass corridor. "Look, behind those hedges is the pool. Did you bring a bathing suit? We can have a swim later if you like."

"Now let's take her to Tante Risha," said Yocheved.

Sara's head was spinning. Yes, she had her bathing suit. She'd figured there might be a pool at school. Now she had to gather her wits and courage to meet yet another new person.

The elderly lady who sat in an overstuffed armchair was listening to a tape while she crocheted what seemed to be an enormous blanket. The minute they entered, she shut off the tape recorder and put her work aside, concentrating her strong, dark gaze on the visitors.

"This is Sara Citron, Tante Risha," said Shira, with an elegant flourish of her arm. "Meet Rebbetzin Bernstein, Sara."

"Doesn't she do this nicely?" said the Rebbetzin, smiling.

"Hello, Sara! Welcome to Montford!" She stretched out a frail, veined hand.

Sara was surprised to find the handshake firm and warm.

"Hi!" she said shyly.

"We'll be neighbors," said the Rebbetzin. "I'm very much looking forward to your company. It will be so interesting to hear all about Jewish life in a place like Dalton, Texas. Has the other girl arrived yet?"

"Not yet," said Shira. "They said she'd call from the bus stop. She was supposed to get in any time after 11. In the meantime, we'll take a quick dip. See you later, okay?"

"Fine. Enjoy your swim," said the Rebbetzin and waved them on their way.

At lunch, Sara met the two youngest children, Ezriel and Naftoli. They would be starting school tomorrow, and Mrs. Rudin was eager to be on her way with both of them for last-minute purchases.

"I'll take the boys for their supplies now, Shira," she said. "When Edie Oppenheim calls, you can drive over and pick her up. I won't be very long, but I would like to get them new shoes if there's not too much of a wait. Don't wander from the phone. We don't want her to feel stranded, right?"

But, as it happened, Mrs. Rudin had gone and returned, everyone had eaten supper, Uncle Meyer had arrived to work in his private domain, and still there had been no word from Edie.

"I'm really getting worried now," said Mrs. Rudin. "This is ridiculous."

She had tried ringing the Oppenheims but, as she had expected, there was no answer. Mr. and Mrs. Oppenheim were supposed to have left for Rochester early in the morning, and Edie, whom they had described as a very mature, responsible young lady, was to have locked up, left the keys with a neighbor, and caught the bus well before noon.

"I wish Tatty were home to help me with this," said Mrs. Rudin. "I can't imagine what's happened."

"Oh, she'll be on the 7:30 bus, you'll see," said Shira. But the tension and apprehension in the air were almost tangible.

"Perhaps you should call the school," Sara suggested. "Maybe they've heard something?"

In a strange way, this dilemma had made her feel like a member of the family. She was already one of them, while the missing girl hovered somewhere out there. But where?

"Good idea!" Mrs. Rudin dialed Rabbi Solomon from the study phone.

"Not a word." she said as she came back into the kitchen. "Oh, I hear the car. That's Tatty. *Baruch Hashem!*"

They were all at the front door when Mr. Rudin walked in.

"Well, that's a nice reception!" he said, surveying the group. "And one extra! So I finally get to meet Sara. *Shalom aleichem* to the Rudin house and to Montford, Sara. So happy to have you here."

"Thank you," said Sara, watching him dump his briefcase and head for the study. He was more like Yocheved, she thought, kind of sandy haired, with a blondish, trimmed beard and glasses. You could tell that here was a busy person.

"Anything in the mail?" he asked over his shoulder.

"No. Just the usual," said Mrs. Rudin. "'Will you come and eat right away, Moish? We have a problem of sorts that can't wait."

"Be there in a sec."

Sara watched as he ate and listened to his wife's story.

"I'd call the clinic," he said. "But first of all, the Oppenheims may be staying at a motel, and who knows which; secondly, I hate to worry those poor people. They have enough to cope with. What a mess!"

"D'you think we should call the police?" Mrs. Rudin asked. She kept running back and forth between the stove and the kitchen table, unable to keep still for a moment.

"Not yet," said Mr. Rudin. "If she isn't here by 8 or 9 o'clock at the latest —"

The phone rang.

Shira was first to answer.

"It's for you, Sara," she said. "One of your friends from Dalton, sounds like."

"Keep it short, dear, please," begged Mrs. Rudin. "We must keep the line free!"

"I'll take it in the den," Sara said. "And I'll make it very quick. Hang up, please, Shira, when I've got it."

From the den she could see the Rudin family, huddled around the table, conferring and gesticulating.

"Hi, Sara!" said a voice. But it was a voice she'd never heard before.

"Hello. Who's speaking?"

"It's me, Edie."

"What?" Sara almost shouted and plopped herself into a black-leather armchair for support. Her legs felt wobbly.

"You heard me. It's Edie. The missing Edie Oppenheim, your co-boarder. Can they hear you?"

"No." Now Sara kept her voice down. "Where *are* you? Everyone here is going out of their mind worrying! And how do you know my name?"

"Easy. When my parents made all these arrangements, the school told them I'd be staying at the Rudins with another 10th-grader, Sara Citron from Dalton, Texas. I figured you'd be there by now." She sounded cool and unconcerned.

"So where are you? At the bus station?"

"No. Listen, Sara. I'm going to hang up in a minute. Just tell them I'm okay, and I'm staying with friends. Not to worry, and not to make waves. Get it?"

Sara swallowed once.

"Give me your phone number so they can reach you," she said.

"No way. Sorry, but for now I'm in hiding. And don't try tracing this call, because I'm at a pay phone, incognito. I'll call again tomorrow night at 8 o'clock. *You* pick up — hear me? If someone else picks up, I won't speak. And I don't want anyone listening in, either. Promise?"

"I'll try, but I can't promise," said Sara.

"Good enough," said Edie. "'I'll be coming to Montford — oh, I dunno, pretty soon. By the way, have you got another name, or just plain Sara?"

"Sara Hadassa," Sara whispered. "And you?"

"Just Edie. That's it." And the phone clicked and went dead.

For a short eternity, Sara sat there, eyes on the little group around the kitchen table, thoughts racing, trying to come to grips with what she'd heard.

Finally she ambled over to the family and dropped her bombshell.

"Trace the call quickly, Moish!" the Rebbetzin said. "They can do that, you know."

"No use," said Sara, and explained about the pay phone somewhere in "no man's land."

"What's so terrible if she wants to stay with friends till school starts?" Shira sounded quite reasonable. "Today's Monday. We have orientation on Wednesday, and then —"

"Okay. Okay," said Mrs. Rudin. "I don't mind if she wants to come a few days later. But we're responsible for her right now! Why doesn't she want to tell us where she is?"

"Well, let's analyze this for a minute," said Mr. Rudin, pushing his dessert to the side. "'She's not totally without conscience, beause she did decide to call. On the other hand, she may only have checked in because she was afraid we might call for a police search, We don't know. She's intelligent, I think. She chose to go the route via Sara. Clever! That's her way of creating an even wider gap between herself and our family — for now, at least. Hmm!"

Yocheved blinked and toyed nervously with the saltshaker. Sara went over to stand behind her chair and squeezed her shoulder reassuringly.

"Don't worry too much," she said to them all, surprising herself with her own boldness. "She sounded fine, really!"

Mr. Rudin made a *brachah acharonah* and got up from the table.

"I'll have to run. I'm late for the *Daf Yomi* already. Faye, let it go for now and see what happens. Some nerve!" He shook his head in frustration, and dashed out to his car.

Chapter Four

A fter Mr. Rudin had left, the girls stacked the dishwasher and then trooped off to the shop — Uncle Meyer's domain — where they properly introduced the new boarder.

The moment Sarah saw him, she knew she was going to like this man. He seemed to be in his late 40s, and although he was certainly older than Rabbi Deutch, he reminded her somehow of him, and of the other men in the Dalton *kollel*.

"I've never had an assistant from Texas before; the Lone Star State, right?" he said. "Welcome aboard! I hope we won't work you too hard. What about the other girl — the one from Brooklyn? Where is she?"

Of course, that opened the floodgates, and they launched into the Edie saga.

"I wouldn't worry overly much about that," said Uncle Meyer, reaching for a jacket to resume his work. "So she wants to stay with a friend for a couple of days. Why not? Obviously, she should have left a number in case her parents call here, but evidently she enjoys being a bit mysterious." He looked at them over the top of his half-glasses and made a face like a sinister spy. Sara giggled.

"Tell me, Sara, do you have *shaatnez*-testing in Dalton?"

"Yes. Now we do. The *kollel* started two years ago, and since then we've had many new improvements. One of the rabbis takes care of the *shaatnez*, and he's also in charge of the Vaad Hakashrus. My teacher's husband is a *mohel*, and lots of people have started taking evening classes with *kollel* rabbis. Ladies go, too." She found she was eager to make them understand that she was not coming from a Jewish wilderness.

"That's fantastic! I'm impressed!" said Uncle Meyer. "But I guarantee you that by the time you go back home, you'll be able to teach that *shaatnez* guy a thing or two. I've got some tricks up my sleeve that I'm almost sure he's never heard of. Anyhow, I guess I'll wait until this Edie decides to show up before I begin to train you in, okay? See you!"

The Rudins had put in a special line for their boarders the year before; and so, when the phone rang on the bedside table right after she had slipped under her covers, Sara grabbed the receiver, knowing it had to be from home.

It was hard to believe that she had only been away from them a day and a half; there was such a tremendous amount to tell them. They were all on the line, Daddy, Mom, and Danny. Sara talked and talked, describing and explaining like a machine that has been set in motion and can't turn itself off.

Finally Mr. Citron managed to clear his throat and get a word in.

"You sound just great, honey! Everything sounds great! Now, listen! We can't keep up this sort of thing. I mean, we can't call every day. So let's say we'll talk once a week, every Saturday night. How's that? And then we'll do a letter once in a while. You too — okay?"

"Sure," said Sara. "And Daddy, please tell Natalie to write."

"I like that Edie kid," said Danny, excitement tinging his voice. "She's got nerve!"

"Well, *I* can't say I share that view," Mom said. "And why is she picking on *YOU*, I wonder. I wish she'd have shown some real courage and spoken to the Rudins. Anyhow, seeing that you'll be roommates, I still hope she turns out to be a nice friend. So write, Sara! And we'll call *im yirtzeh Hashem* on *Motzaei Shabbos*. We miss you and love you. Take care!"

And that had been the gist of it.

On Tuesday, Shira drove Sara all over Montford, pointing out the schools, *yeshivos,* and *shuls.* They dropped in to Uncle Meyer's house, and Sara was introduced. She was getting into the routine quite easily.

But the Montford stores! They were a total revelation. Such a variety of kosher groceries, markets, bakeries, butchers, and fish stores! Shira was aghast to hear that Dalton had only a single kosher grocery, and that *chalav Yisrael* products were brought in for one or two *kollel* families from states up North. There was half an aisle in the supermarket for kosher products, and a small bakery for *challah* and cookies.

"Look at all these clothing stores that actually sell things that we can wear, and book stores with our kind of books!" Sara's excitement was contagious. Shira never let her linger longer than a minute, pulling her in and out of shops, dashing among busy customers, and finally they were in the housewares store. Shira dragged Sara over to a large tank with a kind of fishing net leaning nearby in the corner.

"A *mikveh* for utensils you've just bought!" she said with the flourish of a magician pulling a rabbit out of a hat. "I guess that's as different from Dalton as you can get!" And then, biting her lip and laying her hand on Sara's shoulder, she quickly added, "I'm sorry. I really shouldn't have said that. I didn't mean to make you feel bad."

"Oh, no. This is fabulous! I just can't believe my eyes. I guess living this way all your life, you don't even realize how lucky you are."

'And how easy it is to be *frum* here,' she thought.

They bought some basic school supplies, but Sara decided to wait until after orientation to really stock up on what she'd need.

In the afternoon they'd gone for another dip in the pool. Some of Shira's friends had come over, and Sara, left more or less to her own devices, decided to get back to her room and map out a strategy for tonight's call. But as soon as her head touched the pillow, she fell fast asleep; and when Yocheved called her for supper, her mind was a total blank. She'd just have to play it by ear.

Tonight Mr. Rudin was in no mood for detective stories.

"Tell her, Sara, that she absolutely must talk to us! Her mother called at the office today, and I wiggled out of it by saying I just hadn't had a chance to meet Edie yet. Quite true, but not the truth! We really must insist on having a telephone number, no ifs or buts! Plus, we'd like to know when she's coming." He speared a piece of goulash on his fork and chewed with great determination

Yocheved's thin face was pale. She looked from her father to her mother and then to Sara with a worried frown. She wasn't eating much, and Sara sensed her acute uneasiness.

The two boys didn't appear interested. Their first day at *yeshivah* had already generated numerous worksheets for study. Tonight, all this homework was still a novelty. They finished their meal in record time and were already busy at their desks.

The phone rang at 8:02.

Sara took it, this time in the kitchen.

"Hi, Sara Hadassa!" The voice was familiar now, slightly hoarse, and low pitched.

"Hi, Just-Edie!"

"Are they listening?"

"Yes. Mrs. Rudin's right here in the kitchen, and the two girls, Shira and Yocheved. Edie, won't you —"

"Okay. It's been nice talking to you. I'm hanging up."

"Edie, stop it! Your mother called."

"Sara Hadassa. Take this call someplace where you're alone, and make sure nobody else is on the line. I mean it!" And Sara knew she did!

"Okay, hold on and I'll tell them." Sara pressed the mute button and explained the situation.

"I'm getting very tired of this nonsense. Go ahead and tell her that," said Mrs. Rudin, but she gestured to the girls to follow her outside to the front porch.

"Done!" said Sara into the phone. "I'm alone."

"About my mother?" asked Edie.

"Well, naturally your parents want to know how you've settled in and all that. Can you blame them? Your mother called Mr. Rudin's office, and he sort of got around it without telling."

"Okay. So they won't call again till maybe Friday. Good! You all right? Having a blast?"

"Edie. Please, please, just let us have a phone number. You don't have to say who your friends are — just so you can be reached in an emergency!"

"Sara Hadassa, nice try! But sorry — no! One day I'll explain, maybe. Tomorrow's orientation, right? Who needs it? Not me! Look, tell them that I'll call again Thursday night, same time, and by then I'll know more. Okay?"

Sara gripped the receiver hard. One more pitch!

"They're mad at you. You're putting them into a crazy position. What if they change their minds and won't let you live here?"

"I'll take that chance," said Edie, without a tremor in her voice. "I may have some trouble with the school, of course, but if they kick me out, I'll just stay with my friends and go back to my old school in Brooklyn. No sweat! 'Edie Oppenheim? Straight A's, Hebrew and English; a credit to our institution!' I can just hear Mrs. Heffner, my principal, clear as a bell!" This was followed by a hoarse chuckle.

"By the way," she added, apparently wanting to linger a little longer, "I'm calling from a different pay phone tonight. That's just in case they try the tracing bit. You homesick?"

"No. Not yet. You?"

"No. Of course not! So long! Thursday, 8 p.m."

Sara hung up slowly and joined the others in the evening dusk on the porch. She was surprised to see the Rebbitzen all bundled up in a woolen afghan. The lights in the shrubbery had come on, and fireflies darted to and fro, tiny gold-tipped arrows, tracing their crisscrossing paths on the map of the darkening sky.

"No number," Sara said to the waiting, upturned faces. "She'll call again Thursday evening. Sorry, but I did try!"

"When's she coming?" whispered Yocheved, barely audible against the creaky sound of Mrs. Rudin's rocking chair.

"She doesn't say. But I have a feeling she wants to be here for Shabbos," said Sara, and suppressed the second half of her thought: That is, if you'll have her.'

"This friend is obviously someone she ought not to be with; if not, why no telephone number? I'm going to call her school tomorrow and speak with the principal. This is not what we were led to expect! Tatty will be livid when I tell him." Mrs. Rudin shook her head in disgust, but patted Yocheved's knee. "Don't worry so much, Chevy. It'll all be straightened out soon enough. Get off to bed now; tomorrow's *your* first day of school, and it's bath time for the boys." She got up and walked back into the house.

"I do hope she comes, and I pray that they'll take her in, no matter what this is all about. This girl needs us, even though she doesn't know it," said the Rebbitzen.

"Sure sounds that way," said Shira. "Weird!" She got up and stretched, yawning. "One more morning sleeping late, Sara. We only have to be in school at 10 tomorrow."

Chapter Five

It was Louisa, back from her two-week vacation, who told Sara there was a call for her from Dalton just minutes before they had to leave for school.

Sara grabbed the phone. "Hi, Ma!"

"Sorry, but it's only me," said Mrs. Deutch. "Couldn't let you go off on your first day without wishing you good luck!"

Caught totally off guard, Sara stammered, "Hello! Thanks *so* much for calling."

"Delighted to," said Mrs. Deutch. "Your mother already filled me in on all of your first impressions, and everything so far sounds wonderful, *Baruch Hashem.* So now it's time for the serious part of your adventure: Bais Yaakov. I don't want to keep you; I realize you must be on you way to catch the bus, so I'll just wish you *hatzlachah rabbah,* and give me a buzz if you have questions or problems of any kind. Is that a deal, Sara?"

"*B'li neder,*" said Sara, and added, "Thanks a million, Mrs. Deutch, for making it all happen. Bye!" And she dashed out after Shira, who was already halfway to the corner.

"That was my teacher from Dalton. She's incredible!" Sara said, catching up with the older girl. "Louisa's nice; how long have you had her?"

"She came when Naftoli was born, as a sort of combination baby nurse and household helper, and we've never let her leave. She's here five days a week, from 7:30 till 4 o'clock, and on Thursdays she stays till 8 or 9 in the evening. She does just about everything except the cooking; my mother does all that. She's very attached to the family, and the truth is, by now we all depend on her."

"She told me she comes from Portugal, and at home they speak Portuguese — I mean her and her husband and the kids. But her English is very good!" said Sara.

The girls at the bus stop were all from the Willow Ridge area. Today they were wearing whatever they wanted because this was just orientation day. Starting tomorrow, they'd be dressed in uniform, and Sara would feel different until hers could be ordered and delivered. Shira made introductions.

"Hmm! Let me see," she said, scanning the little group, "who's for 10th? Mirel, you're a Sophy this year, aren't you?"

A short girl with a sweet smile nodded.

"Good. So you take Sara under your wing, okay? Sara, hang onto Mirel. She's been in Bais Yaakov since kindergarten. She really knows her way around!"

Sara felt a little like a package dropped off at the post office, as if Shira was saying, "I've carried it this far; now I'm leaving it in your competent hands." Shira was a great girl; she had done everything that a welcoming hostess could do, and it was because of her that Sara felt so much at home already. But, Sara realized the time had come when she must reach out to her new classmates; and so, when the bus pulled up, she quickly settled down next to Mirel, who seemed quite eager to become her newest source of information.

"We'll be going on some kind of trip today," she told Sara. "The G.O. is picked at the end of the school year, and then they have to come up with something special for the first day in September. Last year we went apple-picking! What do you do at the beginning of the year in Texas?"

"Nothing except a short assembly," said Sara, casting her mind back to the recreation room in the basement of the *shul* where the fluorescent light burned all day. Dense shrubbery outside blocked any daylight that might have filtered in through the few little windows high up in the walls.

They had all been sitting in two rows, boys on one side and girls on the other, while Mrs. Deutch welcomed them to the second year of Dalton's Akiva High School. Her heart quickened as she remembered how excited she and Natalie had been, and how they really hadn't minded the dingy shabbiness of the cavernous room. Accordion partitions had been installed during the summer to divide the two classes, and now Mrs. Deutch was encouraging them to decorate their half of the room in keeping with the theme of the year, which was to be the introductory *Mishnah* of *Pirkei Avos*: "*Kal Yisrael yesh lahem chelek l'Olam Haba ...* Each Jew has a portion destined for him in the World to Come..."

What was Mirel saying? Apple-picking? Nothing could have been further from Sara's mind on that first day of school a year ago. She had felt like a builder, a mover, an iron link in a newly forged chain that she and her friends had helped to carve.

Nevertheless, she listened and nodded, watching as the bus stopped at various locations to pick up more and more girls, until there wasn't an empty seat left. Finally they pulled up at the school.

The auditorium was large, bright, and airy, with a beautiful stage at the far end.

"Last year we had 26 girls in our class," Mirel said.

"There are all kinds of rumors that we're getting another four or five in 10th. Hi, Deeny! Come and meet Sara from Texas! Here, I kept a seat for you. Oh, there's Rabbi Solomon."

Sara only managed a cursory glance in Deeny's direction as everyone rose and the assembly got under way. Teachers stood along the walls or sat with their classes. Sara, overwhelmed by the sheer number of students, drew back into herself and wished she were invisible. Strangely, for a fleeing moment, her thoughts flew off to Edie. Would she ever surface and join her here in this wonderful school?

Rabbi Solomon, she had been briefed, had been the principal here for many years. He certainly projected a strong image of authority, but you could tell that he was very popular and that the girls trusted him. One can sense things like that, Sara thought, and with a happy sigh, she sat back in her chair and relaxed.

After a brief talk about the month of Elul and the upcoming *Yamim Noraim,* the rabbi welcomed all new students, assuring them that they would very soon feel at home here. Sara blushed, sensing that many eyes were upon her, but already they were being instructed to wait for some announcements from the G.O. A roll of drums, followed by a deafening burst of music, nearly shot Sara out of her seat. What now?

Four girls dressed as sailors appeared on the stage. A whistle blew and they stood at attention.

"Sailing into the New Year," they announced in a chorus and immediately went into a dance-gymnastic routine while the girls began to clap enthusiastically in time to the rhythm.

"That's this year's new presidium," Mirel whispered. "See, there's Shira!"

And to Sara's utter amazement, it was Shira Rudin who walked over to the lectern. So Shira was president of the G.O., and she hadn't even mentioned it! Sara couldn't believe her eyes, and admitted to herself, with some amusement, that she couldn't help feeling just a little smug for somehow belonging to this girl, who was announcing the morning's activities with great poise.

After davening in their classrooms, Shira said, they would collect their new books and receive the combinations for their own lockers. Then, at 11:30, the buses were scheduled to leave for Ferndale. Arrangements had been made with a family named Seeberg, who owned a farm there, to have a cook-out picnic lunch, followed by games, at their place. After that, there was to be rowing and canoeing on the nearby lake.

"We promised you we would go 'sailing into the new year,' " Shira said with a grin. She smiled straight at a girl in Sara's row.

"And since Simmy Seeberg in 10th grade is their very own niece, we're sure to get V.I.P. treatment!"

Sara could never remember exactly when she had gotten separated from Mirel after the assembly, and had inextricably become tied up instead with a girl named Shaindel Halpert.

Somehow, Shaindel took Sara in hand and doggedly stuck to her self-imposed role of the new girl's 'best friend' for the entire day, until it was actually time to board the homeward-bound buses.

Shaindel, earnest and well meaning, had a suffocating effect on Sara, keeping at bay others who might have been fun to be with but who remained aloof when they saw that she was not alone. Sara decided to grin and bear it; at least she wasn't left out in the cold.

In the canoe, Shaindel kept up an incessant monologue, pointing with her oar at various other boats and delivering a string of short biographies of their occupants.

"See, that's Simmy Seberg. Her uncle and aunt have the farm, and that's Elisheva Marcus with her in the boat," she said. "They're closest friends. Simmy, between you and me, had a real problem stuttering for years! But she's wonderful now, completely cured! Amazing, isn't it?"

Sara's head was spinning. Wasn't that *lashon hara?* But even if it was, she wasn't going to say so. Maybe if she kept quiet, the silence might rub off on Shaindel. She'd loved the cook-out, and was beginning to understand the advantages of this type of program for the first day of the school year. Obviously, the new ninth graders were quickly absorbed into the high-school orbit, kids got reacquainted after a two-month separation, and teachers melded with the students in an easy social setting. She had heard some call it an 'ice breaker,' and it really seemed to serve that purpose.

Elisheva and Simmy waved their oars in salute.

"Isn't this great?" Simmy shouted. "Hey, get a load of those baby ducks!"

Shaindel swiveled around to get a better view and lost her balance. In trying to right herself, she let go of her oar and reached over too far to retrieve it. Plop! She was over the side, shrieking for help.

For a panicky two-second eternity, Sara thought she'd capsize, but with iron resolve, she managed to steady the canoe, calm the hysterical girl, pull her back in, and steer them back to the dock with her one oar.

Shaindel, dripping wet but beaming now, made sure that the entire school heard every detail of this rescue in record time, and that was how Sara achieved fame on her very first day in Bais Yaakov of Montford.

Chapter Six

Sara was the kind of girl who loved school every bit as much as vacation. She had always excelled in her studies, made many friends, and, to her real dismay, was often favored by her teachers. Naturally, it had been one of Mrs. Citron's favorite pastimes to attend P.T.A. conferences, at which so many other parents often fared dismally. She would sit back and allow the flood of compliments about her 'lovely daughter's' outstanding accomplishments to wash over her. Then she would return home and report to the family that it had all been most enjoyable and invigorating — everything a mother could wish for!

Now on Thursday, her first regular day of classes at Bais Yaakov of Montford, Sara coasted along, buoyed by a tremendous zest to listen, learn, absorb, and enjoy. It was the sort of challenge she liked to meet head on. Mirel had kept a seat for her right next to her own, with Deeny, her alter ego, on her other side. Unflustered by the frequent offers of 'Shaindel the Rescued' to be of assistance, Mirel steered Sara through the day and through the building, showing her where and how to store her belongings.

When Shira came to make sure she was all right during the first recess, Sara was holding court under the huge oak tree, sitting on the grass with the rest of the class, answering questions about her school and life in general in Dalton.

On the bus home, Sara realized that she hadn't thought about Edie Oppenheim the entire day. Walking up the hill from the bus stop, she decided to broach the subject to Shira.

"If Edie tells me on the phone tonight that she wants to come for Shabbos, do you know whether your parents will let her?" she asked.

"For Shabbos, yes, definitely. They'll have to get to the bottom of this whole story and then decide how to go on from there. This kid may be a real case. I hope not — even for *your* sake, because you'll have to share a room with her. Depends on what it's all about, I guess. How was your day?"

"Great, *Baruch Hashem*! The Hebrew was hard, but they're holding off with the tutoring for a while. They want to see whether maybe I can manage without." Sara smiled shyly, casting a sidelong glance at Shira to see whether the older girl had thought she was boasting. But Shira seemed delighted and eager to hear more. "The afternoon was okay; no problem," she continued. "The girls are really nice, and Mirel was super!"

"Sounds good," said Shira as they turned into the driveway. All the windows were wide open to the late afternoon sun, and someone was playing the piano.

"Oh, Yocheved's started her lessons," said Shira. "That's our teacher playing. She's excellent! Her name's Mrs. Ben Ami. Listen!"

She stopped in her tracks, and the two girls stood and listened.

"Wow!" breathed Sara.

"Yes. She's something else. We both take lessons once a week, and of course we have to practice every day. But, like now, she sometimes plays pieces for us just to help us understand and feel what we're aiming towards. Do you play an instrument?"

"No." Sara shook her head. She let Shira go inside and remained by herself, with the sun on her back, soaking it all in — the flower beds, the music, the fullness of her day, and the sensation of being showered with an overabundance of blessings from above. And then, like a sharp stab to her heart, the sudden, cold fear: Edie. Would she ruin it all?

"When did she say she'd call, 8 o'clock again?" asked Shira at supper.

"Yep," said Sara. Nobody had anything else on their minds.

"I remember once, oh, about 15, 20 years ago, in Toronto," said the Rebbetzin between spoonfuls of vegetable soup, "we had a young girl from —"

The chimes of the front door sounded through the house.

"It's those kids collecting again. Why they always come at suppertime I can't imagine," said Mrs. Rudin. "A little more soup, Moish?"

There was some conversation from the hallway, and then Louisa came into the kitchen.

"It's that Edie you've all been waiting for," she said with a twinkle in her eye.

The eight people around the table froze. For a moment they sat, spoons in midair, mouths gaping, all staring at Louisa, motionless, exactly as in a tableau. Then Naftoli scrambled off his chair and raced to the front door. Ezriel, not to be outdone, chased after him, and one by one the others followed, until only Mr. Rudin and the Rebbetzin remained stoically at the table, trying to preserve some shred of normalcy and determined to hold on to their dignity.

With the sun streaming in from the open door behind her, throwing her face partially into shadow, there stood in the doorway a slight young girl, a suitcase at her feet and a duffle bag slung over one frail shoulder.

"Hi!" she said in a low, raspy voice. "I was planning on coming tomorrow, but — whatever — hope you don't mind if I'm a bit early." She shrugged the strap of the bag off her shoulder. It landed on the floor with a heavy thud.

"Well, hello!" said Mrs. Rudin, with much emphasis on the second word. There were bright red splotches on her neck that Sara had never seen there before. 'Hives, indicating severe nervous tension,' she imagined Natalie commenting in a stage whisper. Natalie, the aspiring physician!

"Actually, we've been expecting you since Monday, you know, so you're not exactly early," Mrs. Rudin finished with an artificial-sounding chuckle.

Edie just stood there, saying nothing. Her pale eyes flickered from one to the other, until they came to rest on Sara. And then, almost imperceptibly, she winked at her.

Sara looked away. Edie's special greeting had made her feel disloyal to the others. One flick of an eyelid — but it had spoken volumes! 'You and I are in cahoots here. We belong together. It's us against them, right?' No. She didn't wish to align herself with this girl. If there were going to be two sides here, she'd rather be on the home team. It was all wrong somehow.

She turned on her heel and walked back into the kitchen.

"*Nu?*" asked the Rebbetzin.

"It's Edie, all right," said Sara, collecting the soup plates.

"So what's she saying?" asked Mr. Rudin. "Please give me the next course, Sara. I have no time for all these dramatic goings-on. I'm late again for *shiur!*"

Everyone trooped into the kitchen, and while Sara served Mr. Rudin, Mrs. Rudin made the necessary introductions.

"Moish, here's our long-lost Edie at last," she said.

Mr. Rudin looked up from his plate and met a blank stare from a pair of very light eyes. Unperturbed, he said, "*Shalom aleichem!* Welcome, Miss Oppenheim, and I'm glad you've finally made it. Okay, now I have to run to a *shiur,* but I expect to be back at about 9:30. My wife and I will want to have a little talk with you at that time. Why don't you just join the family for supper now? It's a long way from Brooklyn." He managed to smile in Edie's direction. 'Or from wherever,' he muttered under his breath and concentrated on finishing his dessert.

Sara laid another setting, and Mrs. Rudin, with a worried frown, served Edie her meal. Yocheved had not taken her eyes off the newcomer. Sara thought she was literally scared of her. She wished she could somehow reassure the timid girl.

"Wanna see our turtle?" asked Ezriel.

"Okay," said Edie, taking two spoonfuls of soup and leaving the rest.

"I think I know some girls from your school," said Shira, trying hard to be sociable and friendly. "The Feldingers?"

"Sure. Russi and the twins," said Edie, as if the subject bored her to tears. She looked over at the Rebbetzin.

"Hello!" said Mrs. Bernstein. "I'm *mishpachah,* and I live here too. In fact, you, Sara, and I will be the closest of neighbors. Sara, after Edie's all finished, maybe you'd like to show her your room?"

"Good idea," said Mrs. Rudin. "You don't seem very hungry anyway, Edie. Louisa will clean up in here tonight."

There was no way out of this. The ball was in Sara's court. They *bentched,* and then, carrying one of the bags, she led the way, with Edie at her heels.

"I'm expecting a phone call in about 10 minutes, at 8 or so, from a mysterious missing person," said Sara as she glanced at the wall clock in their room. Edie shut the door and grinned.

For the first time since she'd appeared in the hall, her face took on a lively expression, and those flat, empty eyes were sparkling!

"Hi, Sara Hadassa!" She kicked off her shoes and flopped onto the nearest bed. "Sorry to crash in on your paradise. What is this place, anyway? A single family home or a camouflaged facility for needy girls? That middle child, the fair one with the glasses. She's a problem for sure. Scared? Oh, boy! Did she think I'd eat her up alive?"

"Yocheved? No, she's fine, just shy," said Sara. "By the way, that's *my* bed you're lying on. *You're* living over here! This is your half of Paradise!" And flinging open the doors of the extra closet, she told herself, 'And if you're so sure I'll do you the favor of asking why you're here early, or what you're all about, you'd better think again.'

Edie smiled and made no move to get off the bed. Now she was sitting cross-legged, hugging her bony knees with sticklike arms, her straight, reddish hair hanging like thin curtains on either side of her small, pinched face. Her eyes were large, and so light in color that for some strange reason, it made you uncomfortable to look at her directly. She had pale skin, freckled profusely, and a short, straight, pointed nose. When she felt threatened, Sara thought, that face closed up; but now that she was relaxed, the eyes were flecked with lights and warmth, and the lips parted to reveal a smile of great charm.

"Well, do I look like you thought I would, Sara Hadassa?"

Sara blushed in spite of herself. She realized she'd been caught staring.

"Um. Well, I imagined you more with a slouchy felt hat, dark glasses, a raincoat with the collar turned up, gun in hip pocket, and smoking like a chimney. So I guess the answer is no."

"Real bad guys look more like me — normal, sort of, I think. But *you* look exactly how I pictured you, only more so. A tall, blonde, capable, out-of-town type. No nonsense and nice. I'm glad!"

Edie uncurled herself and got up to stretch.

"I guess there's not much use getting unpacked until things have been resolved in the 'master's' study. Who knows, I may still have to move. So how about you taking me to the *shaatnez* place they told my parents about?"

"Okay," said Sara, wondering when she'd finally get to tackle the huge pile of homework waiting in her schoolbag.

Uncle Meyer welcomed Edie with a great sigh of relief.

"*Baruch Hashem!* Now we can get down to business. Instruction session *Motzaei Shabbos* at 9 o'clock sharp. Work begins Sunday evening. Okay with you two? And you, Miss Oppenheim, have already had your first four days' paid vacation, haven't you?

"Agreed," said Edie, surprisingly, with a grin. "But I'll quickly make up for lost time, you'll see. I respond to hard labor like a parched man to water."

Uncle Meyer listened and nodded. "Is that so?" he asked in a voice tinged with mock awe. "In that case, young lady, we'll promise to pile it on!" He chuckled and waved them off. "See you! Take care!"

"A wise man, and one with a sense of humor," commented Edie. "There's a pool out there, right?" She indicated the dark hedge through the glassed walkway.

"It's gorgeous!" said Sara. "Hey, I think Mr. Rudin's back. I'll drop you off at the lion's den. Good luck, Just-Edie! I think I hope you stay."

Chapter Seven

Sara never discovered what exactly transpired that evening in Mr. Rudin's study.

"Let's leave the door closed on that one," Edie said when she came to their room later that night. "For now I'm staying, and Rabbi Solomon has agreed to forget my late start. Actually, it's only Wednesday and today that I've missed. Big deal!"

Sara, bent over her English reading assignment, cocked her head and raised her eyebrows quizzically. 'It's not the number of days,' she thought. 'And what's more, you know it!'

"So now I'm taking a shower, and into bed. It's been a *very* long day," Edie said. She made short shrift of the unpacking and was under her covers, showered and with her hair still dripping wet, in the time it took Sara to finish her work and pack up.

"You'll like the school," Sara said in the dark. "It's a big school but no so humongous that you'd become a number. The kids are real nice; so far, so good. Of course, I can only compare it to Dalton, and maybe your school in Brooklyn was even better —"

"I doubt that. This place has a great reputation all over, I have to admit. Tell me about Shira."

"Oh. She's G.O. president, and I didn't know that until she walked over to the mike on Wednesday to make some announcements. That says a lot about her, I think."

"Hmm. Interesting! By the way, I like the Citron family on the dresser. What's your brother's name?"

"Danny. How many in your family?"

"Eleven kids last time I counted. I have three older brothers dorming in *yeshivos,* and then yours truly. We divided the rest of the kids with my aunts, and my mother's best friend took the baby." Edie yawned. "Sorry, but I'm zonked! See you in the morning!"

She burrowed into the soft linens, and the last Sara heard was a chuckle from the other bed: "First-class motel! Certified Triple A."

Sara lay a long time listening to the soft breathing of her strange roommate. She had never had to share a room before, and the presence of another person at night felt almost like an invasion of privacy. Of course she'd been to camp and slept over with friends; but that was different somehow. That was always temporary; Edie, in the bed beside hers, was staying. Sara decided that this was going to be a challenge. She would have to try to learn how to cope with it.

Unable to sleep, she played her night game, recalling the supper scene which had been interrupted by Edie's sudden appearance. She knew there was something insignificant and yet arresting that she wanted to zero in on. By concentrating very hard, she was finally able to focus on what had initially drawn her attention about Edie. The girl had worn a most unusual, striking silver necklace, with a pendant composed of a cluster of miniature bells. Sara held her breath. She was positive she'd seen it in the front hall, bright and intriguing against Edie's black T-shirt, and noticed it again at supper. But not since! 'Try to remember,' she said to herself. 'Had she worn it when we went in to see Uncle Meyer? No.' She was almost sure. 'Nor since! Oh, well, what difference did it make, anyway?'

Slowly, Sara repeated the few *pesukim* they had been asked to memorize. She didn't get stuck. Good! She knew them well.

Finally, long after midnight, and still wide awake, Sara *davened* to Hashem, in English, to help Edie adjust to her new life in Montford, and learn to live with a smile.

"I didn't bring a bathing suit. Didn't think I'd need it," said Edie. "Besides, I can't swim."

"You *can't swim?*" Sara was shocked. Back home you swam like a tadpole when you were four or five.

"You heard me," Edie said with a shrug. "But I'll come down there and watch you."

"No," said Sara, very determined. "I'll go ask Shira for an extra suit, and we'll teach you. It's even written someplace in the Gemara that it's important to know how to swim." And without waiting to hear Edie's glib and probably sarcastic rejoinder, she dashed out of the room.

It was Friday afternoon and 88 degrees, perfect swimming weather. The morning had gone quite well, with Edie sitting in the back of the classroom, not making waves. It had been too stuffy and humid to exert extra effort, and the girls, after a few half-hearted overtures, had mostly just left her to Sara, knowing the two stayed together at the Rudins.

Sara couldn't wait to get into the water.

The pool had an unusual oval shape, with a set of steps at either end. Tall, unclipped hedges all around separated it from the rest of the property. A multicolored flagstone path, dotted with beach chairs, encircled the pool, very much like a setting holding a sparkling jewel.

Yocheved had brought the Rebbetzin and settled her in partial shade at the deep end, where one or two maple trees had been planted near the pool.

"We've only got till 4," Shira announced from the diving board. "Then it's boys' time."

She liked to dive in and swim one full length under water before coming up for air. Sara followed on the board, and Yocheved, eyes squeezed shut, jumped in from the side, holding her nose.

Edie settled herself on the stones at the Rebbetzin's side, and after a few minutes Sara climbed out and joined them.

"I hope Mrs. Rudin will come out for a short dip," said the Rebbetzin. "It's too hot to be standing over that stove all day. Have you heard from your parents, Edie?"

"Not yet. They'll call after 5, their time, I guess. It's cheaper."

"How about phoning some of your siblings before Shabbos?" suggested the Rebbetzin. "I'm sure they're all a bit homesick right now." Absent-mindedly she caressed the beautiful, thick, leather *Tehillim* in her lap. "Shabbos and even *erev* Shabbos are always the hardest, I know," she said softly.

"I agree," said Sara, twisting her ponytail tighter in its rubber band. "And not only for the one that left home, necessarily. My mother's going to have a hard time this Shabbos without me there. I just know it. Maybe they'll all eat at my teacher's house."

"People are so much more hospitable out of town," said the Rebbetzin thoughtfully.

"I've heard that many times, but I just can't believe it's true," said Sara. "Look at these Rudins! Okay, Edie. You ready?" She jumped to her feet. "Let's go!"

"I'll indulge your happy dreams, Sara, but I'm warning you, I'm *not* the athletic type. I'll never learn."

"Never say never," the Rebbetzin called after them, and Sara suddenly remembered the words of her English teacher in Dalton: "Don't get into the habit of using platitudes. Don't use cliches in your writing. They're pests that eat away at the garden of beautiful prose!"

"But they're so true, and everyone's used to them," Natalie had argued.

"But they're tiresome and banal," the teacher had said. "Please look that word up for homework." And they had.

The Rebbetzin seemed to have a veritable treasure trove filled with neat little sayings and overused phrases. And yes, sometimes it was a bit much. But so far, Sara had not seen the slightest sign of impatience with the elderly lady. Even the little boys ran to fetch and carry for her. Sara knew she would have lots to write to Mrs. Deutch about her new family.

Edie cooperated with faint enthusiasm during the swimming lesson — that is, after a lengthy "getting wet" procedure. Sara prodded and persuaded her to hold onto the side rail, stretch her arms full length, and — horror of horrors — lift both legs from the floor to kick hard! In this embarrassing position, Edie soon lost some of her aplomb and became almost human. Sara, sensing the shift in power, took the lead and kept her kicking.

"Now do it with your face in the water," she shouted from the side. "No! Don't bend your elbows! Keep your arms and legs straight. Hey, Yocheved. Swim over here and watch her for a minute, okay?" Maybe Yocheved would lose some of her fear of Edie if she was suddenly put in the position of coach!

Some friends of the girls came through the hedge to join in the swim, and by the time they had to leave the pool Edie confessed that she might become a swimmer one day after all.

"I thought about the Rebbetzin's suggestion while I was kicking for my life," she told Sara. "She's got a point. Do you think Mrs. R. would mind if I made all these calls?"

"Ask her!" said Sara and thought: 'When you need a favor and ask for it and get a yes, it has to bring you one step closer to the other person. Wow, a psychologist in the making!' "And while we're at it, let's offer to help for Shabbos. It's Friday afternoon and we're loafing. It doesn't feel normal."

While Sara and Yocheved set the table in the dining room with the most elegant china, silver, and crystal Sara had ever touched, Edie made her calls, and she was on hand when her parents checked in from Minnesota. Shira was out in the back, cutting flowers for the many vases that were placed throughout the downstairs room to enhance the Shabbos.

"We have one flower bed especially planted as a 'cutting-garden.' Our gardener, old Mr. Simpson, makes sure that as the seasons change, we always have fresh flowers out there for our 'Sabbath,' as he call it. Shira likes that job and she's good with flowers; wait till you see her arrangements!" said Mrs. Rudin as she handed Sara the tall, ornate candlesticks for the sideboard. "That looks fine. Why don't you two get ready for Shabbos now? It's getting late. Thanks for helping!"

In their room, Edie told Sara that preliminary tests on her father had confirmed that her parents would have to remain in Rochester for at least three months, possibly longer. Edie's mother was terribly anxious about her children, and Edie, having just spoken to all of them, was able to calm her down. Everything was *b'seder.* They were okay.

"My mother's the worry, worry type," she told Sara while they were getting dressed. "She's the kind that gets upset when she sees a skinny robin, for goodness' sake! 'Don't go here! Don't go there! Don't do this! Don't do that! I'm afraid this will happen or that will happen.' It's pathetic! Why d'you think none of us swim? Same reason!"

"And your dad?"

"Well, he's not worried. He's just — oh, never mind. Right now, hopefully, finally, he's getting the best medical attention there is out there. And it's going to be torture for him to take orders and cooperate. Very hard!"

She chose a garish orange top and matching skirt that fell in tiers and flounces all the way down to her ankles. Silver hoop earrings and silver bangles on both wrists completed the outfit.

"Well, Sara Hadassa, I don't look like your typical Boro Park Bais Yaakov girl, do I?" Edie's huge, light eyes mocked Sara.

"I wouldn't know, would I?" Sara answered, unperturbed. "I'm just waiting to see what you'll put on your feet. Silver high-heeled sling-backs, or what?"

"Wrong! This goes with flat leather sandals. Sorry!"

Although Sara felt tempted to suggest that yesterday's silver necklace would have rounded things out nicely, she resisted the impulse. There was something taboo about that necklace, something secretive. Why?

The phone rang, and it was Uncle Al and Aunt Lisa calling just to touch base, say Good Shabbos, and ask how Cinderella was adjusting. There was a lively dialogue, with promises to meet soon and a "Thanks again for all you've done" from Sara.

In her blue cotton two-piece outfit with large mother-of-pearl buttons running down the jacket, she checked herself in the full-length mirror. A bright, freshly blow-dried blonde mane, held back with a wide headband, framed her flushed face. Did she look too 'Dalton' for Willow Ridge, Montford? She yanked off her glasses and polished them with the hem of her skirt.

"Let's go, Just-Edie. I guess the Rudins are stuck with the weirdest couple of boarders they've ever hosted. *Licht bentchen* is in five minutes!"

Months later, when Sara looked back and remembered that first Friday night at the Rudins', she always relived her sense of wonder and warmth: wonder at the many guests who sat around the long table, interacting with the family and one another as if they had belonged there for ever; and the warmth that was expressed in the beautiful *hachnasas orchim,* the *zemiros,* the Shabbos meal, the flowers, the conversation, and *divrei Torah* from father, guests, and children.

She herself had been one of those guests, and so, of course, had Edie, but she remembered having felt very much an observer, a spectator. Even when she had helped Shira and Yocheved in the serving and clearing away of dishes, she had watched and tried to absorb everything. Like a child mesmerized at a magic show, she hadn't wanted to miss a trick.

In the meantime, some of those guests from that first Friday night had become old familiar faces. Like Mrs. Kellman, the elderly widow who ate with the family every Shabbos and always sat next to her friend, the Rebbetzin. The newly married Russian couple still came occasionally, as well as the inevitable *meshulachim* from out of town who were in Montford for Shabbos and stayed with the Rudins as a matter of routine, and who looked very much like one another.

And Edie? What had she thought? She had answered in monosyllables only when she was directly addressed, her cool gaze skimming over the scene, lingering nowhere. Once in a while Sara had felt a tug at her skirt, a little kick in the shin, under the cover of the tablecloth; Edie's signaling of an implied partnership between the two of them.

But it had been many hours later, deep in the middle of the night, when Sara had finally begun to enter Edie's real world.

Chapter Eight

Sara was dreaming. She was sitting on the grass under the giant oak, trying to get a handle on the *Ivris* homework. It was tough going. This was where she lagged miles behind the rest of the class; *Ivris, dikduk,* conversational Hebrew, and all of that. But she'd get there; she'd plug away at it. Someone was trying to talk to her. It was very annoying. She shooed the person away like a pesky fly, but after a moment the someone was back, talking a mile a minute.

Whoever it was wasn't even making sense. The words were a bunch of gibberish. Sara knew it wasn't a foreign language — Russian, French, or anything like that. It was English all right, but it came out twisted and garbled. She dropped her book and strained hard to understand. There was an urgency in the voice, and even fear. Somehow she felt she had to shake herself awake — to respond — to —

She opened her eyes and was instantly wide awake. The room was bright in the moonlight and silent. Suddenly a torrent of words erupted from the twin bed next to hers.

Edie was talking urgently, incoherently, tossing about and scrunching up her bedclothes. Sara stared. The girl's eyes were open and looked panic stricken.

"No!" she shouted. "Don't!" This was followed by another string of agitated blabbering.

"Edie?" Sara was petrified. "Edie?" she repeated, a little louder. There was no response, no sign of recognition.

Sara tiptoed out of bed and gently nudged Edie's shoulder.

"Edie!" she persisted, trying to rouse the girl from her nightmare or whatever dream world she was in.

Edie sat up and angrily shrugged her off. Her eyes remained vacant and unconnected. Another few words, unintelligible, escaped her lips, a little less wild now and not quite as tortured.

"Come, Tammy," she said and smiled.

With a big yawn, she stretched, turned her pillow around, and lay down, perfectly still, breathing normally and sleeping peacefully.

Sara collapsed onto her own bed, totally spent. That was more than just a bad dream; she was sure of that. Edie was haunted by something. Was it terror of what was happening to her father? She had certainly given no sign of being overly upset about him during the day. On the contrary; she seemed relieved that he was getting the best attention available anywhere. Who was Tammy? A sister? A friend? Someone who tied in with her secrets?

Sara slept fitfully for the rest of the night. By Shabbos morning, she had decided not to mention the episode at all. If Edie would remember any part of it, she'd likely ask. But nothing was said, and Sara pushed the incident to the back of her mind.

Shabbos was great. They went two blocks away to a beautiful shul with a ladies' balcony.

"We hike two miles, not two blocks, to get to services in Dalton — each way, that is!" Sara told Mrs. Rudin, who was walking with the girls. There was a bar mitzvah that week, and Sara listened in awe as the young boy recited the long parshah and haftarah flawlessly. A lavish *kiddush* followed, and then they went home for lunch and a nap.

"I doubt if I'm going to be able to fall asleep now," Edie said. "I slept like a log last night, hours and hours. I think I'll read. Got something interesting?"

Sara kept quiet. She found a copy of the latest Horizons magazine for Edie. "Have you seen this one yet?" she asked. "There's something in there for everyone. Have fun! I'm zonked; I couldn't fall asleep last night for the longest time." If Edie wanted an opening, she'd handed it to her on a silver platter. But Edie obviously had no idea of what had occurred.

Later in the afternoon, Mirel came by with some of her friends to pick them both up, and Edie, at a loss for a convincing excuse to beg off, tagged along with Sara. The girls gave them the royal tour of Willow Ridge, and Sara was astounded to hear that practically every single home in the area was owned by shomer *Shabbos* families.

"Do any of you live in North Montford?" she asked the girls, remembering Uncle Meyer.

"No. We're all from around here. We have our own B'nos for the younger kids, and most of us are leaders. It's not that we don't have loads of friends who live down there — you know Deeny, for example — but it's a big *shlepp* either way, especially when it's hot like today," said Mirel.

"How d'you get to be a leader?" Sara wanted to know.

"You'll tell Shira, and she'll pass it along. The groups go from 3 to 4 on Shabbosim, and you can organize special activities for Sunday afternoons if you want to."

After *havdalah*, the Dalton call came in. Danny had already left to go bowling with his pals, which gave Sara all the privacy she craved. She felt there was just so much she had to tell her parents that she'd never be able to get to all of it. And then there was the news from home to catch up on! Oh, but it was pure heaven talking to her parents after such a long time.

"Tonight we begin our so-called training in the *shaatnez* lab," she told them. "Next week you'll get to hear what it's like working for your spending money. Rabbi Rudin's *very* nice. It looks okay."

Her family had indeed been invited by the Deutches for the *seudah* on Friday night, but they insisted that they'd missed her dreadfully.

"I just hope it's all worth it," Mr. Citron said. "We'll reevaluate when you get home for Pesach. I still hope you'll be back with us for 11th and 12th grades. Be honest, honey, isn't it super to be so wanted?"

"Don't do that to me, Daddy," said Sara. "It's not fair. We've come this far, and it's even better than I hoped. Of course I miss you all like mad," she ended off with a catch in her throat.

Mrs. Citron came to the rescue.

"What about Edie? Now that she's surfaced, do you get along?"

"You wouldn't call it getting along, exactly. It's hard to describe. She's very, umm, private. But she relates better to me than to the rest of them. I guess she figures both of us are on the outside looking in, sort of. But I'm trying!" said Sara, deciding to skip over last night's experience.

"*Gut Voch!*" Uncle Meyer beamed at them, full of good cheer. He had pulled up two extra chairs and indicated that he wanted them to make themselves comfortable. "Okay, young ladies. This is what I want you to do now. Just sit back and listen well. First of all, you may call me Rabbi Rudin. I realize in this house I'm Uncle Meyer, but I know you'll feel more comfortable with some formality, shall I say? I'll take the liberty of addressing you by your first names. I'm sure that'll be fine with you.

"Before I get to the technical part of this work, I want you to understand that this is not just a job, like selling shoes or being a dressmaker. The truth is that any work done conscientiously and with honesty is good in G-d's eyes. But there are some jobs that are more directly connected to *mitzvos;* for example, the writing of a *Sefer Torah,* which is a *mitzvah* in itself, or the making of *tefillin* and *battim* — things like that. And then there are occupations that help keep others from doing *aveiros.* Let's see."

He stroked his beard thoughtfully and then continued, "It's just like checking your lettuce and vegetables carefully, ever so carefully, to make absolutely sure that no one in your house will eat an insect of any kind. Such a job needs great *yiras Shamayim*. We may be alone; no one is watching, but the *ishah yiras Hashem* will do the task with meticulous care."

Sara listened, fascinated. No wonder he was a good *rebbi;* everything was clearly spelled out. She stole a glance at Edie, who seemed to be paying attention but was keeping her eyes glued to the black-and-white tiled floor.

"Now, with regard to the work here, it's very much like your head of lettuce," Rabbi Rudin continued with a smile. "We must check patiently and thoroughly so that no one, *chas v'shalom*, will wear *shaatnez* because of our negligence. It wasn't always this way in America, but by now most people have learned that they must have their clothes checked for a combination of linen and wool anywhere in the garment. It may be found in the collar of a jacket, the lining of a coat, or perhaps in the thread used for making buttonholes! Occasionally, the material from which the entire garment was made is shot through with *shaatnez*.

"This kind of checking cannot be done by just anyone. It needs someone who has learned the skill of examining, recognizing, and then removing any trace of *shaatnez* from the garment. I went through a rigorous training before I began here, and I must say, the more I see, the more I learn. Okay, any questions?" He sat back and gestured to them to ask.

Edie raised her eyes and looked straight at Rabbi Rudin.

"Do you really think Hashem cares what kind of thread was used to sew these on?" She pointed to the gold buttons on the blazer Rabbi Rudin had been checking when they came in. Even if the words had not implied a challenge, the sarcasm in her husky voice would have been sufficient.

The question lay in the air like a thundercloud — heavy, thick, dark, and menacing. The silence in the room was deafening. Sara watched a small spider scurry across the built-in ledge along the wall.

"Do *you* think He cares, Sara?" asked Rabbi Rudin finally.

"Yes. Definitely!" But it came out kind of squeaky.

"What's your problem, Edie? Can you explain?" asked Rabbi Rudin.

"No problem. Of course I know about *shaatnez,* and I'm willing to work here with you, but you asked, and I'm being honest. How can a thing like a piece of thread be good or bad for a person?"

"How about a tiny bit of bread on Pesach?" asked Rabbi Rudin. Both girls looked aghast.

"I don't mean a great big sandwich. Of course not! But how about just a small piece of crust — one bite?"

"That's different!" Edie shot back. "When we understand the reason or purpose for a *mitzvah* it makes more sense. I just can't get excited about kosher buttonholes."

Sara giggled in spite of herself.

"What do *you* think, Sara?" asked Rabbi Rudin, getting up to fetch a bottle of soda from the little refrigerator in the corner. He found three paper cups and placed them on the desk.

"Here, make a *brachah,*" he said, perfectly quiet and unperturbed.

Sara took a drink, and thought carefully before replying.

"Well, it's all in the same Torah. The stuff we understand, like don't kill, don't steal, and the stuff we don't, like not eating *milchig* and *fleishig* together. To me, it is all Hashem's will. Whatever —"

Edie heaved a big sigh and rolled her eyes. But Rabbi Rudin nodded.

"Well put, Sara. We obey one complete set of rules — those given by the *Ribono Shel Olam,* and that includes *Torah Shebiksav* and *Torah Sheb'al Peh.* Those 613 *mitzvos* were given to us to make us better people and to enable us to earn greater rewards. Don't we all say it many times a day? '*Asher Kid'shanu B'Mitzvosav* — Who made us holy through His commandments.' And it works, Edie! Believe me, it does!"

Edie looked at the earnest face and asked, "What works?"

" '*Asher Kid'shanu B'Mitzvosav*' works. Through keeping *all mitzvos* as best we can, we are made holy, higher, better than the rest of the world. It's a fact! Just look around you!"

He made a *brachah* and took a long drink.

"Now, listen. This is becoming a *hashkafah* class and we have to get down to work. I promise we'll come back to some of this another time, but for right now let's concentrate on the nitty-gritty of how we function here."

Sara uncrossed her legs, and Edie, shaking her head as if to clear it from cobwebs, snapped to attention and listened. They were to man the phone, answer the door, receive the clothes, and enter all pertinent details on a printed form.

"We need a description of the item, name, address, and phone number of the person bringing it in. We also enter all this information in the ledger over there so that we have a foolproof system. Oh, yes, don't forget the date! Very important! Next, hang everything up neatly, with a plastic bag over it, on the 'intake' rack.

"After I have examined a garment and perhaps worked on it, we make note of what was done on these forms over here. I will let you know how to determine the charge. If there is anything out of the ordinary, ask me; I'm here," said Rabbi Rudin. "Sometimes if we have to remove fabric containing *shaatnez,* we supply extra replacement material. Again, you'll enter everything in the ledger, okay? So far, so good?"

The girls nodded.

"Now comes the annoying part," said Rabbi Rudin. "You call and let the customer know the garment is ready. This may well be the first of numerous calls. You won't believe this, but some clothes are *never* picked up! Of course, there are also others who bring in their stuff and want it back yesterday! They hang over me, literally, until they can haul it out of here. When I'm not too busy, I don't mind checking while they wait, but there are times when we're just swamped with work."

"Before a *Yom Tov,* or when there are sales, right?" Sara smiled.

"You bet! That's when you'll both have to do some overtime. When it's a bit slow, I don't mind if you do your schoolwork over in the other room. Just make sure you're always available during those hours. One more thing. It may be a good idea for Shira to draw a map of Montford for you. You're both from out of town, and we do get lots of people who need directions on how to find us. Any more questions?" And turning to Edie, he smiled and added, "But do me a favor and keep it simple this time!"

"Very simple!" said Edie. "Do *we* ever get to work on the clothes? I mean, I like all those tools and things you have over there."

"Yes. You certainly will. You'll learn how to remove *shaatnez,* and after a while you'll become very good at it. When we finish with something, we always attach these neat little labels that say 'Shaatnez free' somewhere on the inside of the garment. Very often those labels alert other people to have their own clothes checked. After that, we hang the clothes on the 'take-out rack,' and of course, we try and do them in order, as they come in."

"Are there any others here in Montford who do this *shaatnez-*testing?" Sara asked.

"Two others. But I must admit that this is by far the busiest of all. Okay, now I'll begin to work on some of the things waiting to be checked, and tomorrow evening, *b'ezras Hashem,* I'll get you both started. I'm happy to have such bright and willing helpers. Thanks for coming tonight, and now, I'm sure you'll be wanting some *Melaveh Malkah.*"

Chapter Nine

Morah Jacobs was the cherry on the icing of the cake; the 10th grade was unanimous on this. Well, almost. One never knew what Edie thought or felt. She continued to sit in the back of the room and kept her own counsel. She stayed put during recess, busying herself with homework or writing letters. Sometimes she just rested her head in her arms on the desk, and whether she was asleep or just tuning out nobody really knew.

Sara, who was rapidly falling under Morah's spell, tried to crack Edie's shell of indifference. Walking home with her from the bus stop, she'd ask, "What did you think of that lesson on *teshuvah* this morning?"

"She's okay," Edie would reply. "Personally, I can take that kind of thing better from an older person. How old is she, d'you think?"

"She's 20. Mirel told me they had her for *mechaneches* last year. Some of the older kids remember her from school, way back. Seems Michal Jacobs was always a big name around here."

Edie sighed. "Listen. She's obviously bright, and I believe she's sincere. She prepares her classes for hours, I'm sure, and she thinks she's got it all down pat. Like two plus two? Four, of course! Things fall down — not up? Gravity, naturally! A *tzaddik* has a miserable life while the *rasha* gets all the breaks? One second, here's the answer — page so-and-so in *sefer* . . . That kid hasn't a clue to what real life's all about."

Sara listened. How old would Mrs. Deutch be? Probably close to 30. Sometimes she found herself comparing the two teachers in her mind, and she had to admit that Edie did have a point. Mrs. Deutch, married with three little children, had left all this behind to help build a new Jewish community in a comparative wilderness. This was only her third year in Dalton, and already she had wrought miracles; she, and all the others like her. Surely that's what Edie meant. Practice in living, exposure to diverse situations, marriage and motherhood, different places and circumstances, different people with varying views — that's what formed a person like Mrs. Deutch.

"I prefer Rabbi Rudin," Edie would say. "I can't say why exactly, but I trust that man!"

"Me too," Sara said, and meant it.

In the evenings they were swamped with *shaatnez* work. Rosh Hashanah was two weeks away, and all of Montford, it seemed, would be decked out in brand-new wardrobes. Rabbi Rudin had rented some extra clothes racks to deal with the overflow.

"After Yom Kippur things will be just as hectic. That's when all the boys come home from *yeshivah,* and they'll be bringing their suits for Succos. It's going to be 'overtime' for you two until after *Yom Tov.*"

In the early mornings, before it was time to get up, Sara would hear the sounds of the *shofar* coming from the *shtiebel* whose property skirted the back of the Rudins' boundary. A special bonus that comes with living here, she thought, like the siren on Friday afternoons to announce the approaching Shabbos. She liked all these things; they helped you 'think Jewish.' The *shofar* turned her thoughts back to Morah Jacobs' lessons on the deep significance of the *Yamim Noraim* and how these related to each of them individually.

"We've covered the concepts of *teshuvah, tefillah,* and *tzedakah* as being powerful enough to avert a bad decree," Morah had said. "I would like to suggest that all of us try for the remainder of *Chodesh Elul* to do something extra in each of these areas."

Sara had found herself stifling a yawn. It was only a week and a half till *Yom Tov.* They'd finished with Rabbi Rudin at 11:30 the night before, and still there was schoolwork and giving a hand to Mrs. Rudin here and there. She had been so very, very tired.

"What I'm trying to get across to you girls is this: '*Lo hamedrash ha'ikor, elah hamaaseh.*' Learning all these things in theory is only necessary because it must lead to deeds. For instance, now that you thoroughly understand the power of prayer, try to select one or two *tefillos* which you will say with special *kavanah,* and allow nothing to distract you at least while you *daven* these few. The more the better, of course. Even we, in one small class, in one remote corner of the world, can make such a difference!" She'd looked around the room as if to touch each of the girls with her own enthusiasm.

And Sara, lying in bed and listening to the last of the *shofar* sounds carried through the open window, thought: 'What was it that Rabbi Rudin had said? That *mitzvos* make us holy and different from all other nations.' Right! She'd concentrate on that particular aspect of the *tefillos.* She would try to remember to say with special feeling each *brachah* that began with the words: *Asher Kid'shanu Bemitzvosav,* and also that part in the Shabbos *Shemoneh Esrei, Kadsheinu Bemitzvosecha.*

Edie's performance in school, both in *Limudei Kodesh* and *Chol,* was excellent. She absorbed and squirreled away all information, and was able to reproduce it on her tests, unadorned and perfect. But socially she was a total failure.

Any chance of acceptance by the girls was finally lost when Edie brazenly voiced her opinion about Morah Jacobs. Not that she actually came out against the teacher. It was during one of those sessions before class when the girls were raving over Morah's most recent wonderful lesson.

Simmy, trying to draw Edie into the group, asked for her input.

"She's okay," said Edie with a shrug and a face that clearly showed her lack of enthusiasm.

"What d'you mean, 'okay'?" said Simmy's friend Elisheva. "She's fabulous!"

"Sorry, but I'm not joining your fan club," said Edie, and she walked away.

Sara felt like taking her by the shoulders and shaking her. Why did Edie have to act this way, making enemies left and right?

The next morning when she walked into the classroom, she saw several of the girls clustered around Mirel's desk. Edie was not yet in the room. She was probably taking her time getting off the bus, finding her supplies in her locker, and slowly making her way to the second floor. She was certainly never in a hurry to begin the school day. When the girls saw Sara, they stopped talking and acted as if they'd been caught red-handed. Sara felt as though she'd been slapped, but it was an awkward situation, and she pretended not to have noticed. With a forced, cheerful "Hi!" she settled into her seat and asked Mirel, "Which is the last day of school before *Yom Tov*?"

It worked! Mirel breathed a deep sigh of relief and pulled out her school calendar, and the two of them studied the next few weeks' schedule.

Sara was pretty sure the class had nothing against her; they'd all been really friendly and helpful. It had to be something to do with Edie, and of course, they assumed that Edie and she were inseparable. 'How ridiculous,' she thought. 'Just because we've been thrown together by fate, does that make us best friends? Okay, so maybe that's my job, my challenge. There's no such thing as "fate." Hashem wanted us to be together, so somehow, some way, I'm meant to tackle this problem.'

Soon enough it became abundantly clear that the girls were avoiding Edie. They simply pretended that she wasn't among them. Sara, on the other hand, was fully accepted as before, but they did not draw her into their evident, if unspoken, pact of excluding Edie. In this one area of her Bais Yaakov school life, Sara floated in a sort of no man's land.

One evening Sara wrote a letter to her teacher in Dalton. In her previous correspondence, she had already apprised her of her new roommate and the mysterious circumstances surrounding her.

בס"ד

Dear Mrs. Deutch, לאי"ט

My life is so very full. I'm constantly thinking — one more thing, one more experience, one more happening, and I'll explode.

A pressing, immediate problem is a situation in school caused by my 'roomie' at the Rudins'. She is being shunned by the girls! They accept me all right, and I think they're a great bunch. But I'm caught between them and a strong urge to do what is really right. I have a strange sense of loyalty to this girl, or maybe it's just the feeling of 'here's a chance to do a *mitzvah,*' or thirdly, it could be the temptation to prove that I can rise to a challenge by being supportive. Whatever it is, I can't join their ranks in this, even though I often feel they are justified. I'm desperately trying to figure out what makes 'E' tick. Alone in our room, she's a different girl. Also, she has admitted that she *does* trust one person around here, and that's the uncle of the Rudin kids with whom we work in the *shaatnez* lab.

Otherwise, I'm having a great time! A girl called Simmy Seeberg offered to coach me in Hebrew language and grammar. She's an A-one student, and I love going to her house anyway. B"H, I'm catching on! The Rudins are wonderful. Thanks for having found them for me!

For the New Year I wish you and the Rabbi כוח"ט, and please forgive me for any wrong I may have done to you during the last year. I'm truly sorry if there was any time I disappointed you.

Sincerely,
Sara

P.S. I'm sorry to bother you with this whole business, but you did ask me to let you know if I had any problems I couldn't handle. Please tell Natalie I miss her!

Chapter Nine / 69

Part Two

Chapter Ten

בס"ד

Dear Sara, עמו"ש
Succos is over, and we're all back in school working hard. I just couldn't find enough quiet time to
concentrate on your problem with 'E,' and rather than dashing off a few meaningless words or making a short, hurried
phone call, I decided to wait until the *Yamim Tovim* were
over to give it the attention it deserves. In any case, I imagine
that there wasn't all that much actual schooltime last month,
so that the two of you were probably thrown together more
than usual at home, whereas there was less contact and fric-
tion with the others.

Have there been any changes in 'E's' behavior? How do
the Rudins manage with her? You didn't say. You wrote that
in the confines of your room, she's a different person. It

seems to me that that might be the ideal time to probe and discover, very gently, what makes her so difficult, and then help her to open up. She desperately needs a good friend! I am certain that the rest of the class will respect you for remaining loyal to 'E' and will not let this interfere in their relationship with you. They know very well that the way they're acting isn't very nice (to put it mildly).

Another possibility would be to engineer a time when 'E' is busy elsewhere and you can speak to the Rudins' uncle alone, and tell him all about the miserable situation in school. Together you might be able to hatch a plan. Good luck!

I'm glad your Hebrew studies are going so well. See, I told you so! Before long you'll be a teacher at Akiva High. I don't doubt it for a minute!

Hatzlachah Rabbah!
Mrs. Deutch

But before Sara had a chance to make any inroads with Edie, two things occurred that brought matters to a head.

The first was another terror-filled night episode, very similar to the one Sara had not forgotten but pushed to the back of her mind. Earlier in the evening — it was a Wednesday — Rabbi Rudin had told them that he would have to be away for a long weekend to lecture on *shaatnez* in three different places. The girls watched him pack his scrapbooks full of material swatches he had removed from garments, along with many other items of interest such as his famous 'museum' pieces — clothes so shot through with *shaatnez* that they could not be repaired. Edie and Sara were to mind the shop, receiving and processing clothes brought in and taking care of routine pickups.

That night Sara woke with a dreadful start. Someone — Edie? — was standing over her, gripping her shoulder in an iron vise, wild with urgency and a desperate force, straining against Sara, who tried to shake herself free to sit up. Torrents of jumbled, incoherent speech, interspersed with the name "Tammy," cascaded over her while she wriggled to loosen the grasp that held her down.

"Come, Edie, come. Time to get back to bed," she heard herself whispering, swinging her legs over the side of the bed and finally prying the fingers off her aching shoulder.

But even in the dark she could tell that those eyes, wide open, did not know her. In them was a palpable fear, without recognition or any sense of time and place.

Feeling her way along the beds and furniture, Edie made for the large double window. More garbled words followed, and frenzied plucking at the curtains and shades. Then, suddenly, there was an almost imperceptible lessening of tension, and the words "Oh, Tammy!" slipped out in a heartbreaking, pitiful tone.

Sara tiptoed over and gently led the girl back to bed. Edie allowed herself to be tucked in like an obedient little four-year-old, closed her eyes with a great, weary sigh, and fell asleep instantly, looking exactly as if nothing had ever happened.

Sara got back under her covers, pulled the comforter way up to her chin, and stared up at the ceiling. She was shivering and sweating at the same time. Her shoulder felt sore to her gently probing fingertips. This was too much for her. It was scary and threatening. How could she feel safe sleeping with this terror-stricken girl? Obviously, Tammy was not some fictional nightmare. There must be someone in Edie's life who had a hold on her, someone she kept hidden, locked deep inside her. Perhaps Mrs. Deutch was right, Sara thought, and she should very simply try to give Edie an opening to tell her some more about herself. If that didn't work, she could always use the alternate route of Rabbi Rudin. Oh, but Rabbi Rudin wouldn't be back till Monday evening, and then they'd be so busy catching up, there'd be no chance to explain the situation to him privately.

"You woke me up last night," she told Edie when they were getting ready for school next morning.

"Oh, yeah? How come?"

"Don't tell me you don't remember. You were moaning and groaning in your sleep. Very noisy! Do you sleep alone at home or share a room with any of your sisters?"

Edie looked at her strangely, and Sara thought she detected a flicker of fear in her eyes.

"Don't remember a thing," she said, and quickly turned her back on Sara, busying herself with making her bed. Then she added nonchalantly, "Sorry 'bout that. Yes, I do sleep with two of my sisters at home, but I guess they're sound sleepers. Anyhow, I don't think I usually do that kind of thing."

Finally she straightened up and asked, "What did I moan about? Any deep, dark secrets?"

"Oh, yes, indeed," Sara smiled. "If I hadn't been so groggy and also mad at you for waking me up, I would have taken clinical notes. Very, very interesting, psychologically speaking." She hoped she was keeping it light enough. "As it was, I just kept saying, 'SSH! SSH!' and some sweeter things like, 'SHUT UP!' " Okay, she'd given Edie her opening.

"Sara Hadassa," said Edie, coming over to where Sara stood in front of the mirror. She looked over her shoulder straight into her eyes and said, "I'm glad you're my roommate for now. I really mean that. Just don't ever change!"

Sara turned around and faced the girl.

"Now, what's that supposed to mean?" she asked.

"Maybe tonight I'll explain, after work. I feel by now I owe you that much. Don't think for a moment that I don't realize that without me there in school, you'd be the most popular girl in 10th grade!"

Sara shrugged. "Oh, don't be silly," she said. "C'mon, let's run, we'll miss that bus!" She tried to hide her excitement; this was the first time she felt she could hope for a break in this quandary.

Shira and her friends were already waiting at the bus stop. All their talk these days centered on seminaries: where to apply, and to how many different schools, the pros and cons of each one, and, of course, Israel versus America or even England. There were also a small minority of girls who were opting to skip all that and go either to work, to college, or to learn some kind of skill after graduation.

Sara and all the members of the Rudin household knew that Shira's dream was to attend Beth Sefer L'mechanchos in Yerushalayim and to return a year later to teach in Montford. The school had prestige and a wonderful reputation, but everyone said that getting in there was like winning a 'gold' at the Olympics. Openings were tightly limited, and applications numbered in the hundreds. Because of this, Shira played it cool with the other girls and repeatedly emphasized that she'd gladly settle for any other seminary, as long as it was in Yerushalayim.

But first things first. There was the concert to organize for January, and Shira, as head of G.O., was already busy planning. She had told Sara and Edie that it would require an enormous amount of work, and that she hoped they'd help her with odds and ends at home.

"Sure, glad to; sounds exciting!" Sara had said, but Edie had refused to commit herself.

"You know, you're crazy," she said to Sara.

"You're just piling it on. What for? 'Yes, I'll do this. Yes, I'll do that.' And now, on top of everything else, there's the Shabbos group."

The Shabbos group indeed.

"I love it. I adore it," Sara said with a huge, happy grin that seemed to reach every part of her being. "It's the best part of the week, definitely!"

When she had applied for a job as a B'nos leader in Willow Ridge, all the positions had already been filled. But shortly after Succos, the Montford J.E.P. organization had opened a new branch in a non-religious neighborhood about eight blocks from Willow Ridge, and Sara had been given the seven-year-olds. She had started out with two boys and three girls, and now there were 11 children who came regularly every Shabbos at 3 o'clock. It was tailor made for her. During that hour (and often longer), she was transported back to Dalton, slipping easily into her old life-style, able to empathize with these youngsters. Already they were saying that Sara was the best leader they'd ever had, and other girls were asking for ideas and tips on how to handle their groups.

Sara and Edie were now both in their room, doing schoolwork. It was the quiet hour before supper and the shop. Sara, who was really studying, sat at the desk, and Edie, curled up in the white wicker rocking chair, was supposedly reading a literature assignment. Instead, she was staring into space.

"My father isn't really," she said suddenly.

"What?" Sara turned to look at her.

"My father isn't really my father," said Edie, and shut her book. "My real father was killed in an accident. He was on his way to *shul* on a Shabbos morning when a drunk driver swerved onto the pavement and hit him."

Sara gulped and covered her mouth with one hand. "Oh, Edie!" she managed.

"Well, I never really knew him. See, there were four of us; my oldest brother was six, the twins were four, and I was almost two. So even the boys say they hardly remember him. Of course, there are pictures."

Sara, unable to utter a word, held her breath and waited. Edie got out of her chair, reached into the back of one of her drawers, and produced a small leather wallet from a yellow manila envelope. Silently, she handed it to Sara and settled back in her chair.

Sara opened the slim album, its leather smooth and thin from age and much handling. 'How often did Edie snatch a moment alone to look at these?' she wondered. First there was a wedding picture of two smiling young people. Sara stared, fascinated.

"You're the spitting image of him," she said in a voice filled with wonder.

"I know," Edie said. "My mother's told me so many times."

There were about a dozen snapshots of the growing little family. The boys first, and then tiny Edie in the high chair, in her stroller, and between the twins, holding their hands and giggling. Then there was one taken, perhaps, at some family *simchah*. All six were grouped by a professional photographer before an arch of flowers, with Edie, all in pink, on her father's lap.

Sara looked up at Edie. Her heart ached for this girl. "What happened next?" she asked.

"My mother had an uncle who was still single. She knew him all her life, and when this happened they decided to get married. Sure, he's much older than she is; as a matter of fact, everyone's always saying how she was born on his *bar mitzvah* Shabbos, but that's okay. You'd never know. Things worked out fine and then along came the rest of the crew."

She walked towards Sara and flipped the little album over to start from the back. Here there was only one picture, again taken professionally. In the center was a man with a grey, square beard, looking sternly at the camera, next to him a woman smiling broadly, whom Sara recognized from before, and a large group of children. Edie was in the back row, looking as if she couldn't wait for this photography-session-nonsense to be over and done with. Typically Edie!

Sara studied the picture long and hard. What she felt like saying was: 'This can't possibly be the reason for the way you behave. For all intents and purposes, this man is your father, and has been since you were a baby.' But instead she asked, "I don't quite know how to put this tactfully, but Edie, you never really knew your own dad, so has this made any real difference? Honestly? I mean, you know — " Her voice trailed off helplessly.

Edie took the wallet from her, slipped it back in the envelope, and returned it to its hiding place. When she was back in the rocking chair with her legs curled under her, she spoke thoughtfully.

"In most ways the answer would have to be no. But, as you've realized by now, I have a will of my own, opinions on almost everything, and that's where we clash, my father and me. I do love him, and of course the kids, but there are areas where we argue and fight — and then, without the slightest shred of logic, I tell myself, 'If he were my real father, we would see eye to eye.' Get it?"

"Sure. But believe me, this has nothing to do with stepfathers. My dad and I had a terrible disagreement about this whole Montford thing. In the end, my mother and I won. Whose side is your mother on when all this goes on?"

"My father's, of course," said Edie, getting out of her chair. "My mother, as I think I've told you, is forever worried about a million things anyway. She always has been, she's that type, and what happened to my own father probably made it much worse. Part of all this is her fear of rocking the boat, imagining all the worst scenarios that could come from such arguments. Like, what will our family come to if the younger ones see Edie arguing with Tatty? etc., etc. Anything to keep the peace!" She sighed. "Anyway, let's go eat. I'm glad I told you."

"So am I. Thanks!" said Sara and followed Edie to the kitchen. They were the last ones to come in, and Sara apologized for both of them. While Shira helped her mother serve the soup, Sara noticed Yocheved's unhappy little face studying Edie. 'She doesn't like or trust her,' Sara thought, 'and she's uneasy about feeling that way. It must be so hard on her, having to live under one roof with someone she wished wasn't there. Maybe if she knew more about Edie, she might feel sorry for her and learn to understand her better.' But the story had been told to Sara in confidence, and she knew she couldn't divulge any part of it.

"I have a surprise for you, Sara," said Mrs. Rudin. "We're going to have another party in our house next week, just like the night you first came, only smaller and more for men."

"Oh, Mommy, another one?" Shira wasn't exactly overjoyed. "They're such a pain!"

"What till you hear for what," smiled Mrs. Rudin. "It's for the Dalton *kollel* — a parlor meeting. Now, what do you say to that, Sara?"

Sara was blushing. She was on cloud nine.

"Wow!" she said. "Really? What's a parlor meeting, and is anyone coming from there?"

"Yes, indeed!" said Mr. Rudin. "I guess they sent you ahead as their good-will ambassador, and you've done a great job. You're a living advertisement for their valuable work!

"A parlor meeting is a way of raising money for an institution. Usually someone speaks about the *mossad,* and people come, have a bite to eat, leave a check, and go on their way. We were asked whether they could have it in our house, and we were very happy to say yes. And you, Sara, certainly had a lot to do with that!"

"They're sending a Rabbi Deutch to speak. Isn't that your teacher's husband?" asked Mrs. Rudin.

"Yes, it is. I'm *so* excited," said Sara. "I can't wait. I know you have a ton of these benefit *tzedakah* events, but for this one I really want to help a lot. Okay? You too, Edie?"

Everyone's eyes were on Edie now.

"For Sara Hadassa, any time," she said and actually smiled.

Chapter Eleven

And then there was the birthday party.

It was Mrs. Rudin's Hebrew birthday that Sunday, and quite unbeknownst to her, everyone at 153 had been busily scheming to surprise her. The Rebbetzin, knowing what the girls were planning, had asked Mrs. Rudin to help her with some bills, medical insurance claims, and *tzedakos,* in her room. This left the coast clear in the kitchen, where the four girls managed to produce what they called a Viennese table. It all looked scrumptious!

The 40 long-stemmed red roses which Mr. Rudin had brought home to mark the occasion were arranged in various tall crystal vases, one of them incongruously placed on the kitchen counter close to where they were now sitting at supper. Mrs. Rudin had waved away all suggestions that tonight they eat in the dining room.

"No way! There's altogether much too much fuss. As it is, 40 feels 10 years older than 39. Let me get used to it slowly," she laughed.

"You're real old, Mommy," said Naftoli. "When I'll be a father, you'll be a grandmother or a great-grandmother, right?"

"Why do you say that?" asked Mrs. Rudin, intrigued.

" 'Cause now you're in your 40s, and I'm just in my sixes," said Naftoli matter-of-factly.

"Okay," said Ezriel. "Let's get on with it." He gave Naftoli a none-too-gentle dig in the ribs, and amidst much clowning and giggling, they both got up.

"Attention, attention," said Ezriel. "Me and Naftoli want to say something."

Everyone smiled and sat back to listen.

"Go ahead!" said Ezriel, nodding encouragement to Naftoli, who quickly produced a grubby-looking scrap of paper from his pants pocket and painstakingly unfolded it. He cleared his throat, and with a wide, toothless grin, he recited:

> "This is Mommy's special day,
> She's the best in every way,
> When we are bad she doesn't yell,
> And when we fight she doesn't tell (not always!)."

Now he nudged Ezriel, who took over.

> "We think she cooks and bakes just great!
> She never makes us stuff we hate,
> We think that she deserves the best,
> So here's a homemade treasure chest."

He reached under the table, and both boys handed their mother a small gift-wrapped package. Sara noticed that Mrs. Rudin's eyes were glistening as she began to undo the ribbon.

"Mazel Tov!" the two screamed in unison, and Ezriel added, "We did get a little help from the Rebbetzin with our poem."

"Not much," said the Rebbetzin. "But I have no idea what's in the package. They wouldn't tell. Such a secret!"

It was a pretty little treasure chest made from popsicle sticks that had first been painted brown. Strips of metallic gold paper resembled hinges and fastenings, and some colored glass beads made magnificent jewels on the domed lid.

Sara had been watching Mr. Rudin, relaxed and smiling at the head of the table. For this special evening, he had arranged with his *chavrusah* to start their nightly *shiur* one hour later and the whole family felt the difference.

"Look, it has its own hinge!" Naftoli shouted, unable to contain his excitement.

"Isn't it wonderful!" said Mrs. Rudin, stroking his hot, flushed cheek. "Now — let's see," she slowly opened the box.

There, nestled in crumpled tissue paper, lay a little mound of shiny, sparkling silver. Carefully Mrs. Rudin untangled it and lifted it up for all to see. It was a beautifully linked chain of small hammered discs, and from its center hung an exquisite pendant composed of a cluster of miniature bells.

Sara stared.

"It *is* a treasure," said Mrs. Rudin in awe.

All the oohing and aahing became just background noise. Sara's eyes swiveled over to where Edie sat. But Edie had risen, mumbled an apology about being too late for work, and had disappeared down the glassed-in walkway.

"Oh, it's beautiful, boys!" said Mrs. Rudin. "Just gorgeous! Thank you *so* much! But where did you get this? Did Tatty or Shira take you shopping?" She gave each of them a kiss and hug.

Sara waited, holding her breath, while Mr. Rudin got up, saying, "No, I had nothing to do with it. But my birthday's coming up pretty soon, so you two pros can start getting busy preparing right now. I like your taste." And with this neat exit line, he quickly made for the front door and his car. "See you all," he called back over his shoulder.

"I had nothing to do with this, Ma," said Shira, puzzled. "Where *did* you get it, kids?"

The boys were standing on either side of their mother, squirming and whispering behind her back. Naftoli shifted from one foot to the other.

"You tell!" he hissed at Ezriel.

"Okay," said Ezriel. "It's a long story. Mommy, the truth is, we found it. You know that old playhouse Tatty got us when Naftoli was a baby? We never use it anymore, right? And anyhow, it's all old now, full of spiders and cobwebs and stuff. But one day on Chol Hamoed, when Naftoli's friends came over to play, he took them back there to show it to them, and they started a whole game pretending it was a real house."

"And I said if it's a real house, then we've got to make a *succah* for it," Naftoli chimed in. "So we started working, finding sticks and wood and branches. And then Shaya was poking under some dirt and leaves to get at a great piece of wood for the walls, and he found this buried treasure."

"And then they called me, and we looked for a name or something, but after a while we figured it's ours, because we found it on our property," finished Ezriel. "We were so excited we never finished the *succah,* and we changed the game to hunting buried treasure instead."

"Amazing!" said the Rebbetzin. "Then what did you do?"

"At night we washed it in hot soapy water in the bathroom, and I kept it hidden in my lowest desk drawer for your birthday, Mommy. It was terrible keeping a secret for so long, especially for Naftoli. He wanted to give it to you a hundred times."

Ezriel loved being the center of all this attention.

"Oh, I forgot, we asked Uncle Meyer if it's okay. Of course, we never told him why we asked, but just like — you know — by the way. And he said it's okay if the people who own a field find something buried there, if it has no *siman,* it's theirs. We looked carefully, and there's no *siman,* just the words 'Sterling Silver.' "

Mrs. Rudin shook her head in disbelief.

"What a find! But you *did* make the beautiful treasure chest especially for this gift, didn't you?" she said. "And it's a little treasure all by itself." She handed the necklace to the others to admire.

"What an unusual, beautiful piece this is; obviously handmade," said the Rebbetzin, fingering the discs. "How strange. Nobody *ever* goes to that corner of the property, not even the gardener! It's an overgrown tangle of bushes. Well, good for you, boys!"

"Didn't your cousin wear something like this when she brought you here that first Sunday night?" Shira asked Sara. "I seem to remember having seen a similar necklace somewhere before. Oh, no, I think it might have been the lady at the printers who are doing our concert tickets and programs. Nice, Mommy; wear *gezunterheit bis* 120!"

"Do they have clappers?" asked Yocheved, examining the little bells. "Oh, wow, they do!" She was enchanted.

"I'd better get off to the shop!" Sara exclaimed. "I bet Edie's already up to her neck with jobs. It was a great party. Mazel Tov again, Mrs. Rudin!" And with this, she dashed out of the room.

Her mind was racing. What to do next? Rabbi Rudin was still away; no help available from that quarter. Should she confront Edie with her knowledge? In the few seconds it took to get from the kitchen to the *shaatnez* room, all she could think was, 'Oh boy! Am I ever in a pickle!'

Edie was at the door, handing a suit and coat to a customer and collecting the money. As soon as the man had left, she crossed off the transaction in the ledger and wrote 'Paid-in-full' with a great flourish. Then she turned to Sara.

"Nice girl from Texas. Good-natured, honest and straight. Very poor actress. No talent for pretense." She lifted her eyebrows and sighed. "Yes, of course it's mine and you recognized it. Mind you, I give you full credit for trying not to let on! You did not look in my direction although your face was aghast, and your eyes were almost popping out of your head. Another thing I admire is your power of observation and retention. Every last person in that room saw me wearing that thing, and you, I think, are the only one who realized it."

Sara plopped down on one of the chairs. Relief washed over her. Edie had taken the bull by the horns; there was no need for complicated strategy.

"Shira did say something after you left. Something about it looking familiar. But she's off on the wrong track," said Sara, waiting now to hear more. Edie was sitting in Rabbi Rudin's swivel chair, the high-intensity light playing on her fingers as they fiddled with the knives and tweezers lying on the green-felt cloth. Her face was thrown into deep shadow.

"Of course, I may be wrong. Maybe they're better actors than you are, and perhaps they *did* recognize the necklace. Mr. Rudin, for example; he's no dummy. I wonder — "

"Who's Tammy?" Sara asked suddenly.

Edie dropped the tweezers and stared at Sara, lips apart. Even in this light, Sara saw the color drain out of the girl's face.

"What do you know about Tammy?" she whispered.

The doorbell and the telephone rang at the same time.

"You get the phone," Sara said, and stepped over to the door. It was Hindy Gross, one of Shira's friends from school, dropping off a skirt with a matching vest in a beautiful color combination of earth tones.

"It's stunning!" said Sara. "Where did you find it?"

"I picked it up at a super-sale at 'Outfits and Such.'

I have a deep hunter-green silk shirt to go with it. Perfect match, no?" She pointed to the dark green swirls in the woven fabric. "Let's just hope this isn't riddled with *shaatnez*. Tell me, do you like Montford? And this job, is it okay?"

Sara noticed that Edie had finished on the phone. She kept her voice calm and answered, "Yes, I love it here, and the job's fine too. Hey, Edie, come look at this outfit. Isn't it gorgeous?" She went to enter the transaction in the 'received' column, and then added, "Rabbi Rudin's out of town until tomorrow night, so I'm not sure when it'll be ready. We'll give you a call the minute it's done. Okay? Bye!"

She shut the door behind the girl and quietly resumed her seat.

"Well?" asked Edie.

"What do I know about Tammy? Nothing at all," Sara said truthfully. "Nothing except that I'm certain she means a lot to you; you're worried about her; and, okay — " She hesitated for a fraction of a second before continuing, "When you babble at night, the name keeps coming through all the gibberish, loud and clear."

"All right," said Edie. The color was back in her cheeks, and she looked somewhat relieved. "Now, listen, Sara Hadassa. There is a Tammy in my life, and you know what? I've thought about this a lot. When Rabbi Rudin comes back and we get a slow half hour some time soon, which, knowing our slave driver, is unlikely," she rolled her eyes and made a grimace, "I've made up my mind to talk about this whole business with both of you. You make an unlikely pair of shrinks, I'll say that much, but you're just what might help."

"Fair enough," said Sara. "But just tell me this one thing; that necklace and Tammy, are they connected?"

"Yep!" said Edie, and would say no more.

Chapter Twelve

Sara did not give Rabbi Rudin advance warning of the upcoming 'session.' She felt that Edie, having come to a
decision to talk, should be allowed to pick her own time
and place.

Nor would he ever be told why he hadn't been able to find the
two-piece outfit for the Gross girl (as he called Shira's friend). He
knew it had been checked and bagged. The call had been made,
but when she came to pick it up the night of the parlor meeting, it
had disappeared off the face of the earth. He had kindly allowed
the two girls to take the evening off to help Mrs. Rudin, and had
therefore decided not to bother them with this. He'd apologized
and promised to search again with the help of the girls tomorrow,
and he was sure it would turn up. Hindy had been very polite about
it, he told Sara and Edie afterwards, and why he hadn't seen it

when it was hanging right there between the two coats for the Wassermans, he couldn't fathom.

Rabbi Deutch came laden with gifts for everyone. Sara's parents, by now, had a pretty good idea of the people in the Rudin house, their approximate ages, and what they might like. Mrs. Citron had gone to town on this! She missed Sara badly and said in her note that shopping for them had, in a funny way, brought them closer together.

There was a beautiful knitting bag in brightly flowered chintz for the Rebbetzin. It was attached to a collapsible wooden frame that could stand on four spindly legs next to her armchair, holding yarn, patterns, and whatever she was currently working on, or it could be folded neatly for carrying about the house.

A recipe book entitled *All Our Favorites,* just published by the Sisterhood of Akiva Day School as a fundraiser, was enclosed for Mrs. Rudin. And for the man of the house, a large, black-leather luggage tag that, instead of the usual address blank, contained a hand-calligraphied *Tefillas Haderech* to hang in the car, and the same in a rich, dark brown for Rabbi Rudin.

For Shira, Yocheved, Sara, and Edie there were four matching nightgowns in a fine pink-and-white striped cotton. Each was embroidered with the appropriate name on the collar.

"Wow! These definitely call for a midnight feast at 153 Willow Ridge Drive," Shira said. "How about this coming *Motzaei Shabbos?*"

"Can we come?" Naftoli whined.

"Only if you have pajamas to match," said Yocheved, bursting with pride at having been included with the older bunch.

"Oh, you've got better gifts than silly old pajamas," said Sara, handing them each a beautiful set of Lego.

Even Louisa hadn't been forgotten. She beamed when she saw the bottle of cologne.

"Sara, how did your mom know this is my all-time favorite?" she asked.

Sara giggled. "You won't believe this, but I once told my mother that you smell like home 'cause you use the same scent she likes. I guess she remembered." She was flushed and felt proud of her parents for having chosen all these presents that were such a success.

There were also letters from home, one from Mrs. Deutch and a very special one from Natalie, signed on the back by every single student and teacher in Akiva High.

Sara and Edie had helped Mrs. Rudin to set up. The dining room looked as though a caterer had just left; it was arranged to perfection. There were trays of hors d'oeuvres, fruit arrangements, cakes of every kind, cookies, drinks, and desserts. In the living room several rows of chairs were set up, with a lectern for the speaker. Flowers, in abundance, graced every available surface.

Sara couldn't remember when she'd last managed to change at such lightning speed. One last glance in the mirror, and she was ready to dash out. Edie, still in the shower, yelled above the sound of running water for Sara to go ahead. She'd be there in a minute.

Rabbi Deutch was scheduled to begin at 9. Now, at 8:30, there were small groups of men milling around, tasting the delicacies and enjoying each other's company. Mr. Rudin and two of his friends who had helped in the planning of this affair were conferring, and Sara watched as several of the people came over to them and handed them checks or envelopes. She went into the kitchen to help Mrs. Rudin mix the punch.

"You look very pretty," said Mrs. Rudin. "Is that a new sweater?"

"Uh-huh," said Sara. "Mom sent it with Rabbi Deutch. Will all these people stay to hear him speak? And do you think there'll be lots more?" She sounded anxious, she knew, but hadn't Mr. Rudin said that people at parlor meetings mostly just left their checks and went on their way? She did so want as many people as possible to hear what Dalton was all about — the schools, the *shuls*, the *kollel*, the small group of families who were working so hard to build a *frum* Jewish community and succeeding beyond their wildest expectations. All this he would talk about, she knew, because his "community *kollel*" was a powerful link in that chain. Perhaps the *most* powerful when you stopped to think about all the various services that these six couples rendered to the people in the community. And that was besides the Torah that they studied there every day and far into the night!

When Rabbi Deutch finally began to speak, she figured there were about 30 men sitting and listening. Tall, straight, and thin, with a thick black beard, he made an imposing picture. Having been a Shabbos guest in his house so many times, Sara knew him well and could tell he was really enjoying this, eager to launch into his presentation. He, just like Mrs. Deutch, had been born and raised in the New York area. It was easy for him to paint a picture for his audience of the enormous contrast between Montford and the place he called home today.

By now there were easily 50 in the audience. Sara hung onto the rabbi's every word and did not notice Edie coming into the kitchen from the walkway. When it was over, she went limp with relief and joy. It had been super so far, and the bell was still ringing. It would certainly be a financial success, said Mrs. Rudin, and Sara secretly patted herself on the back, hugging to herself the knowledge that her presence at the Rudins' home had had just a bit to do with it. Mr. Rudin had said as much, hadn't he?

Suddenly Edie was standing right in front of her, and Sara's knees buckled.

"Oh, no!" she gasped.

Edie grinned and pirouetted all the way around, preening as if for a fashion show.

"Hindy's?"

"You got it!" said Edie. "Like?"

"You're crazy! Get that thing off you!" Sara hissed.

"May I ask why?"

"One million reasons. But just for a starter, what if her father's here?" Her eyes searched the crowded living room. Who on earth did she think she was looking for? She'd never seen Mr. Gross in her life!

"Don't be ridiculous!" Edie was saying. "Fathers don't know what their daughters buy. And anyhow, this could be a coincidence; same dress, different size." She flicked an imaginary speck of lint from the vest.

"Oh, yeah?" said Sara. "And what if she wears it next Shabbos? I'm assuming you're not planning on stealing this dress, and that she'll somehow get it back. And what if Shira says, 'Oh, nice! That Oppenheim kid has exactly the same outfit.' What then?"

"Sara Hadassa, have you ever thought about becoming a mystery writer?" Edie peered at her with X-ray eyes.

"I give up," Sara said, exasperated. "You're totally off the wall, and how you'll sneak this outfit back on the rack once you've spilled soda all over it, I can't imagine. But — like you said, you've got your own set of values and ideas. You're 'Just-Edie.' "

Edie swung her freshly blow-dried hair away from her freckled face.

"Exactly. And you — you have absolutely no sense of adventure or daring. What's *your* idea of fun? By the way, you haven't said how you like it on me."

"Rabbi Rudin would kill you if he knew. Let's hope he never finds out. Fun!" said Sara and walked away.

"Texas has no sense of humor," Edie retorted, firing her parting shot.

Luck was with Edie in several ways. Call it *mazal!* Hindy Gross picked up her outfit the following evening with no one the wiser. Mrs. Rudin often wore her 'buried treasure' with great pleasure, and in absolute ignorance of its history. And, in a different league, and best of all, Edie's father's doctor had assured Mrs. Oppenheim that unless anything unforeseen cropped up to snag the progress, Mr. Oppenheim might well be home by January.

In the meantime, Shira applied to three different seminaries in *Eretz Yisrael,* dutifully enclosing $75, non-refundable, in each. She had felt very tempted to make it $100 for B.M.L., her favorite, but, as she confided to Sara, Edie might have had the nerve to do such a thing but not she. *Chaval!* There was nothing more to do now but pray and wait.

In the last week of November, a snowstorm — which was almost unprecedented for that time of year — hit the Northeast. Montford was buried under 12 inches of pristine white, and it was still coming down. Sara, who had never seen anything like it, could not tear herself away from the windows. Dalton's winters consisted of two months, December and January, when the temperature might hover around 30 degrees; there was never any snow! The scene outside was something she might have seen on a postcard or maybe in *National Geographic Magazine,* to which Danny subscribed, but never the real thing like this!

All schools had been canceled, and even Mr. Rudin had decided to stay home. There was no point in trying to dig out from under until the snow actually stopped falling. The boys, drunk with joy, rushed out into the backyard, muffled up to their eyes in layers of warm, waterproof clothing. Equipped with snow shovels, they were ready to build the biggest snowman of all time. Sara, watching them from the kitchen window, felt her excitement mounting. She wasn't going to miss any of this! Shira, amused and thrilled that her beloved Montford was once again scoring high marks with their favorite boarder, outfitted her in her own winter clothes, high boots and all. So it was Sara who became the snowman's chief sculptor, and the boys her slavish assistants.

That evening, Edie talked.

Chapter Thirteen

By early afternoon it had stopped snowing. All over Montford the plows were out, clearing the main roads first and gradually reaching the small side roads and cul-de-sacs.

In the evening when the girls came to work, they found Rabbi Rudin already peering through his microscope and then deftly removing tiny fragments of material from the lining of a collar with a special hand vacuum.

"Hi, there!" he said. "We won't have many customers tonight, I guess. I'm going to be able to really catch up on these." He gestured in the direction of the 'take-in' rack. "Why don't you two get busy with some of your schoolwork, and — "

"Rabbi Rudin?" Edie pulled up an extra chair.

"Yes?" He asked, vacuuming up the last traces of the offending fluff with great concentration.

Edie's voice sounded low and husky and just a little less brash than usual. Sara, holding her breath, waited.

"Can we talk?"

Rabbi Rudin gave the collar a few determined strokes with a small wire brush, folded the garment, and laid it aside.

"Talk?" he said finally, looking up at Edie. "What about?"

"Me."

Rabbi Rudin glanced up at the wall clock wistfully, as if to say, 'There goes my beautiful extra work time'; but then he swiveled around to face Edie.

"Sure," he said with a smile. "I assume by 'we' you mean the three of us?"

"Uh-huh," said Edie, nodding.

"Fine; time out!" said Rabbi Rudin. "Sara, get some Snapple from the fridge and fetch another chair. We may as well be comfortable."

Sara, watching Edie closely, sensed the girl's suppressed agitation. She was fussing with her hair, and her light eyes, darting from one to the other, seemed sparked by inner turmoil. Her restless hands toyed with the tools scattered on the green-baize matting of the desk.

"Shoot!" said Rabbi Rudin, looking at her with great kindness.

"Okay," said Edie, addressing herself to him. "I've been planning to tell you some of this stuff for a while. Sara knows. But I figured this would be a good time because of the snow, and no one coming — "

Rabbi Rudin crossed his legs. "Right. Why don't you start at the beginning?"

"I will," said Edie. "Okay, Sara already knows that my father's really my stepfather. He's an uncle of my mother's who married her when my own father was *niftar*. I was almost two at the time, and there are three older brothers, and now there are 11 of us, *kein ayin hara*. The big boys all dorm in *yeshivos*, so that leaves me at home with the rest of the kids."

She looked at Rabbi Rudin. "Is it too confusing so far?" she asked.

"No. I think I get it. Very sad about your father. How did it happen?"

Edie told him about the shocking incident and then continued. "I don't get along too well at home, and it's going from bad to worse. School's okay. My schoolwork's never been a problem, and I stay away from close friendships. Most kids don't like me much anyhow; I'm too different." She said this nonchalantly, as if she were describing someone else. "So I mostly stick to myself. Once in a while I discover another rebel like me, and we hang around for a bit. But nothing to last, you know?"

"What about home?" asked Rabbi Rudin.

"Home. Let's see. I hate all the rules and regulations, but most of all, the limitations. See, my father's the owner of a large carpet and flooring place, and he has a bunch of people working for him. There's no arguing with him. He gives the orders, and whoever doesn't toe the line is out in the street that very day! No pardon, no second chances. And it's a lot like that at home. 'You do as I say, quickly, no discussion.' My mother's perfect for him; she's happiest when she's told what to do. Some people want that kind of life, I guess."

"Go on," said Rabbi Rudin, swishing the ice around the remains of his drink.

"My older brothers are mostly out of it, although we've lived through some doozies on *Yom Tov*. The younger kids? Who knows? It may turn out all right for them or it may not; it's hard to tell. There's an eight-year-old boy who gets plenty of *petch*! He doesn't obey easily, and he's already in trouble in school. But I can't worry about him; I'm in too deep myself right now!"

"Hmm," said Rabbi Rudin. "Maybe you could give us some examples of what goes on?"

Edie flexed her fingers.

"I'll try. But first I want to say that my father's a terrific person. He's the most honest human being I know. The other day my mother told me that he gave up a huge deal last year because there was something a little bit shady in the customer's office records. He happened to discover it and immediately refused the contract. What I'm trying to say is, he *is* strict with everyone, but strictest with himself. And now, with this awful sickness, he's unbelievable. No fuss, no pampering! He wants to be on top of it, and he's sure, *be'ezras Hashem,* he'll be okay.

"But you see, I have ideas too, and I'm stubborn, and we just don't agree. I feel that everything in my house is negative. I've thought about this a ton! Many parents let their kids do just about anything they want. I guess they're too permissive. But on a scale of most permissive to most forbidding, my parents must win top prize for the no-no's."

"I really got myself into hot water one time. You know those wooden signs you put on your front door that say '*Mishpachas* so-and-so'? Someone brought us one from *Eretz Yisrael:* '*Mishpachas Oppenheim.*' One night I stuck a piece of paper over the Oppenheim part. It said: *Lo!*" Edie giggled.

"What don't they let you do?" Sara couldn't understand.

"Anything; you name it. No sleeping over at a friend's. No shopping sprees with other girls, ever! We belong home! No extracurricular activities in school. It's more important for us to stay home and help our mother. 'Who needs all that nonsense,' my father says. 'Let's get out priorities straight!' He wants miniature *Eishes Chayils,* or should I say *N'shei Chayil?* And besides, I'm treated exactly the same as my 12-year-old sister! Fun in our house consists of going to a cousin's *chasanah,* or baking for company! That's fine for some, but it's not working for me. Oh, I dunno. Am I making sense?"

"Have you ever told your parents how you feel? I mean, when you're not screaming at anyone," Rabbi Rudin smiled. "Just reasonably, quietly?"

"I've tried. It's no use. We're not the 'round-table-conference' kind of family. That goes for anything. We don't do stuff together, period! And anyhow, my parents don't seem to understand that kids, just like all people, are different. I come off being the 'bad one' just because I like to prove that I'm Edie. Like, I have questions, for instance, about my father's accident. Here he was on his way to *shul,* and this happened. Nobody wants to talk about it or discuss what it all means. I fight and argue and slam doors to shake the house! And other times I just clam up; don't talk and don't answer anyone."

Sara couldn't help comparing her own life at home with what she was hearing.

There were long outings with Natalie to the malls, swimming, bowling, and walks after B'nos on Shabbos with all their friends. There were camping trips with her parents and visits to museums and concerts. They had Shabbatons and speakers, special *shiurim*, and Shabbos invitations to the homes of the *kollel* families. And of course, there were community picnics and family *melaveh malkahs* at the *shul*. She could barely imagine a life as Edie pictured hers.

"Tell me," Rabbi Rudin was saying. "How do you feel about life here at the Rudins? Is there greater freedom in this family?"

Edie thought about this for a moment.

"It's hard to compare two such different setups. I mean, look at this place! But still, I think I'd have to say yes. Shira has more fun than I'm allowed. These kids go to camp, for one thing. None of us have been allowed to go, and it's definitely not a matter of money. They take music lessons; they're always out with friends, even Yocheved! And anyway, nobody's bugging them all the time. Mr. Rudin leaves them alone, and Mrs. Rudin isn't afraid of her own shadow. She's confident enough to give them space.

"I mean, let's take clothes. I've come in Friday nights dressed like — well, not like your average Montford Bais Yaakov girl. Nobody said, 'Boo'! It's sort of like I've been testing them, and they won the contest. They really did!" She smiled.

"I see," said Rabbi Rudin. "By the way, how did you come by those clothes? I assume you've never worn them at home."

"You bet I didn't! I'll get to all that in a moment." Edie got up and paced the room nervously. "My father has Crohn's disease, which is *very* painful. He suffered from cramps and ulcers in the stomach and colon. Ultimately, he developed inflammations, infection, and fever. He needed a first-rate surgeon to relieve the obstructions with a major operation. Things looked very serious and of course, I began to feel it was all my fault. Everyone knows that ulcers are mostly caused or aggravated by tension and I know he's totally frustrated with me; he's just not used to being disobeyed. I would see my mother looking at me with big, reproachful eyes everytime I started acting up. And yet, with all that guilt piling on, I couldn't stop.

"And then I got to know a girl one grade above mine. Her parents are Israelis, but they've been in this country about 10 years now. Her father drives a taxi, and her mother works in some pizza place. They're *shomrei Shabbos* and they keep a strictly kosher home, but that's about it."

Edie stopped pacing and resumed her seat. She turned to Sara and said, "Listen carefully, Sara! We're coming to Tammy now." Sara licked her lips and nodded.

"Her name's Tamar. Here she calls herself Tammy — more Americanized. She's a beautiful girl, and I'd seen her in school, of course, but we just never really met because of the difference in age, I guess. She began telling me about her life, and I told her about mine. These people live in a very small apartment in Boro Park, and they're trying to 'make it' in the U.S. They work like crazy, saving for the good things in life, as they see them. Tammy comes home to an empty house every day, and the same for Sundays. I felt drawn to her, as if she were a magnet and I were a pin.

"Many times I asked my parents to let me invite her over, or to give me permission to go to her place for company, but by the time they'd grilled me on her *yichus* and *frumkiet,* she was strictly out! I begged and pleaded. I tried to explain how much she needed a friend, and that maybe we could influence her for the good. No way! And, as usual, no explanations, no discussion, just, 'No! And that's final!'

"So then I began telling lies. I invented class meetings, and extra projects in school so we could stay late and *schmooze.* I talked hours to her on the telephone, without mentioning her name. I really liked her. But most of all I adored the feeling of independence and decision-making, of flying!

"The day my parents told us about Rochester, I made up my mind. Somehow I'd swing it; I'd move in with Tammy. I made it clear that I wasn't going to be sent to some relative, and so it was agreed that I would board here and go to school until my father could come home. The last morning — it was a Monday — I was to leave our key with the neighbors and take the next bus to Montford. And, as you've guessed, I went to Tammy's house instead.

She had slipped me her extra house key, and I let myself in. And then we began our four-day fling.

"Tammy's mother had known I was coming. There was the second half of Tammy's hi-riser, so I had a place to sleep. We took something to eat the first morning and left the house. We ran around and 'hung out'; we played pinball machines in the arcades in Coney Island and spent hours staring at fish in the aquarium, sometimes just the two of us, and sometimes with friends. That night I called here from a pay phone for the first time and got to know Sara.

"Tuesday was our first day of school in New York. Tammy decided to play hooky in honor of my visit. She assured me she'd done it before lots of times and had gotten away with it. As to her family, Tammy's father was so tired by the time he came home nights that we barely saw him. Her mother's a kind, easygoing type. She told me to have fun and take it easy. She had no idea, of course, that we weren't going to school. Cousins and friends drift in and out of that household when the parents are home. They smoke endlessly, talk Ivrit, and make plans about what they'll buy and do when they can afford it."

The phone rang. It was Rabbi Rudin's mother, checking in from the West Side. It seemed New York City had not been hard hit by the storm. Rabbi Rudin began to describe the weather scene in Montford.

Sara sighed, stretched, and got up to look out at the quiet snowy darkness while Edie rummaged in the fridge for more drinks.

Rabbi Rudin was saying that it was a very slow night for the *shaatnez* lab, and that he would be going home soon.

When he hung up, he nodded to Edie. "Yes, Edie. I'm with you."

"Okay," Edie continued. "On Wednesday Tammy took me by subway to the Village. You know, where they have all these boutiques — jewelry, art stuff, and way-out clothes and antiques. And then — hold on! — she showed me how she shoplifts. I was so nervous, I thought I'd pass out. I knew it was stealing, but I was up to my neck in this now, and I watched without letting on to others what I was seeing, if you know what I mean. She has it all figured out, down to a science, you could say. Big hobo shoulder bag, fingering things, sliding them down into the bag, and quickly looking at the next pair of earrings. Or she would drape a scarf around her shoulder, walk over to the mirror to study the effect, and then just leave it on, strolling outside to the next shop. We divided the loot at night. She threw in several outfits of hers that she wasn't wearing anymore — my present Friday-night wardrobe!" Edie grinned.

"Of course, it was terribly wrong, and we both knew it, but as the saying goes, forbidden fruit tastes sweet.

"And so, with the music blaring away on her C.D. player, we sat on the beds decked out in the stolen goods, and I argued with her. I told her that she couldn't pretend that this wasn't stealing. But she had answers for everything. 'Those people are a bunch of no-goodniks. They're all into drugs down there. They know there's plenty of shoplifting and that's just part of their business expenses. No sweat! Live a little! Don't start giving me *mussar* now, or let's forget the whole thing.' It was wild!

"Okay, I gave in, and we went again on Thursday. Different block, same kind of shops. I hadn't taken anything for myself yet, just watched Tammy out of the corner of my eye. Then I saw that necklace with the bells. Sara knows about that; I'll explain in a minute," she said aside to Rabbi Rudin. "I slipped it over my head. I was standing in a dark corner of a tiny jewelry store, and the only saleslady there was showing someone a tray of rings in the window. I pushed the pendant inside my shirt and continued on as if nothing had happened. It was that easy! At that moment I saw the cop. He was standing right behind Tammy and watching her slip something into her bag. 'Run, Tammy, run!' I know I mouthed the scream, but no sound came from my lips.

"There were loud words back and forth, and he accused her. The saleslady started shouting in a foreign language, gesturing and tearing at Tammy's hair. The policeman pushed the woman aside and concentrated on what Tammy was saying. She tried to charm her way out of it, but she was caught. I saw him arrest her and drive her off in his police car. All this had taken no more than maybe eight minutes. Tammy had not spoken my name or even looked in my direction. That's the kind of friend she is!

"Somehow I got back to her place, threw my stuff together, and headed for Montford. Yes, I left her a note, but I'd didn't say much in case her mother found it. By the way, they let her go. I've been in touch, and she was reprimanded with a severe warning. Her parents were called down and had to sign that they'd be responsible for any misdemeanor. Phew! Even telling it makes me break out in sweat!" Edie shook her head.

"You've arrived late for school here. How come Rabbi Solomon admitted you anyway?" asked Rabbi Rudin, ignoring the whole incredible tale.

"I told the Rudins that first night that I'd stayed with a good friend, even though I knew my parents didn't really want me there. I knew it wasn't right, but I promised them that now I'd be a good girl and stay put. Maybe they guessed more than they let on, but they certainly decided to let me stay. They took a chance on me and even talked Rabbi Solomon into doing the same.

"I wanted nothing more to do with stolen goods, so the Sunday after I got here, I buried that necklace in an overgrown corner of the yard. Ezriel and Naftoli found it on Succos, cleaned it up, and gave it to Mrs. Rudin for her birthday."

Edie stood up, took a big, sweeping bow, and announced: "THE END!"

In the silence that followed, both girls watched Rabbi Rudin, whose eyes were fixed on the far wall. Sara thought he was never going to speak. Seconds seemed like minutes. In her extreme uneasiness, she once again got up and walked over to the door to gaze at the snowy wonderland out there, washed silver-white by the light of the street lamps.

"Are you very shocked?" Edie broke the spell at last.

Rabbi Rudin came back to earth and cleared his throat.

"No. Not really," he said, stroking his beard thoughtfully. "You're normal. You have your *yetzer hara;* we all do. You gave in to it, as we all do, unfortunately, now and then. Right, Sara?"

"Uh-huh!" Sara did not trust herself to say more. *She* was certainly shocked! Lying! Deceiving! Running away — shoplifting! Edie was just too much for! And yet —

"The question is," Rabbi Rudin continued, "why have you told us all this now? You could easily have cruised along until you returned home. No one would have been any the wiser. So why?"

Edie looked from one to the other and ran her fingers through her hair.

"I guess I just had to unload, y'know? Well, actually, there are two parts to it. First, it was just getting too heavy to carry all by myself. And then, I think I need help to figure out where to go from here."

"Good!" said Rabbi Rudin with a warm smile. "Two excellent reasons, and part one's already accomplished. You've shared your burden with Sara and me, and that's the first step towards part two. Now — where do you go from here?"

He got up and stretched.

"I suggest we adjourn this meeting, and you, Edie, will have to do some homework. Think about this carefully. Where would *you like* to go from here? And also, perhaps, should there be any kind of action regarding the necklace or Tammy? Sara, anything you'd like to add?"

"I've got an idea," said Sara, who had been cooking up a plan in the back of her mind. "But for now, I'd rather just think about everything, okay?" 'Not only that, but I know more about this than she told you,' she thought.

"Sure. And Edie?" said Rabbi Rudin, getting into his coat, cap, and muffler. "Let's agree that the two of you will not discuss any of this until we resume the conversation right here. Is that all right with both of you?"

"Fine," said Edie. "And thanks loads! I can't tell you how — "

"Then don't try!" said Rabbi Rudin, smiling. "Hope the car starts! 'Night!" And he was out the door.

Chapter Fourteen

They had promised not to discuss the matter, but this put an unnatural restraint upon them as they were getting ready for the night. After what had just transpired, any other topic, it seemed to Sara, would sound superficial and hollow, but total silence was an uncomfortable alternative. And so she chattered away about Shira's upcoming interview with the B.M.L. principal, who was now in the States to select the lucky elite, and did Edie think she'd be accepted? And since everyone said the snowstorm had been unusually early in the year, did she think it would all melt quickly? And would Edie mind testing her on some of the material for tomorrow's Navi test?

Edie's replies were mostly grunts, and finally a yes; she'd give her 10 minutes to go over the Navi questions together.

When they were both in bed at last, each lay silently, though

Sara could only guess at what was going on in Edie's head. She realized that she had not played her old "recall" game for a very long time. Squeezing her eyes shut tightly, she willed her mind to focus on the scene in the *shaatnez* lab.

There they were, the three principal players in this evening's drama, grouped around the main work area of Rabbi Rudin's domain. To Sara, that lamp-lit world had become very dear. When she was in that room for any reason during the day she found it cold and lifeless; but in the evening hours, with Rabbi Rudin snipping away at his work, the phone ringing off the wall, people coming and going, and the small talk of friendly exchanges, it was a pulsing warm hub of activity. And Sara often reminded herself of that first talk they had had with their boss; their work was an activity of the greatest importance to every Jew!

Tonight, the glistening snow outside and the unreal quality of isolation had made the room even more snug and safe, like a polar bear's den or an igloo, she thought. And so, Edie's revelations had fallen on friendly ears and hearts, warm and supportive, nonjudgmental and patient.

Edie's revelations — yes! One couldn't exactly call that monologue, Edie's 'confession.' Was she really sorry? Wasn't snitching Hindy's outfit another form of shoplifting? Sure, she had slipped it back on the rack early the next morning, but then, the necklace could also be returned to its owners in Greenwich Village, and Edie seemed to have no compunction about that. Perhaps that first experiment with jewelry had made taking Hindy's outfit easier.

Aveirah goreres aveirah, one sin leads to another. Hadn't Mrs. Deutch taught them last year about this very thing? Why does one *mitzvah* inevitably lead to the next one, and the same for *aveiros*? In both cases the initial act may be difficult, but it paves the way for a second time, and another, and another, which are now easier by far. And so begins a chain of behavior which gathers momentum, making it even harder to turn back and do *teshuvah*. Probably in this case that's what had happened. Edie, in fact, had looked upon the dress episode as a lark, a joke, an adventure. And if she'd felt any guilt about the necklace, she certainly hadn't been one bit bothered about taking the outfit! She'd even blamed Sara for being a killjoy and a stick-in-the-mud! Rabbi Rudin, of course, would never hear about all this.

Goodness! What would Natalie say? The thought of her old, trusted friend instantly brought on a tidal wave of homesickness. It was so sudden and strong that Sara actually felt a heavy, painful pressure in her chest. She gulped and swallowed hard to keep herself from sobbing.

Stealthily turning her head to check on Edie, she felt a sharp stab of jealousy to see the rhythmic rise and fall of the quilt, indicating that the perpetrator of all this upheaval was fast asleep.

The injustice of this opened the floodgates; and Sara, burrowing deep under her blankets, gave way to her pent-up feelings and cried and cried, until it seemed there were no more tears to shed.

The next morning things looked a great deal brighter. A brilliant sun made short shrift of the snow on the main thoroughfares, and as the early commuters began their steady stream of migration from Montford to the big city, slush quickly turned into slick black asphalt. But for Sara, by no means ready to part with all this glorious snow, the side roads were still packed, hard and white. Drifts of snow had formed high piles along the sidewalks, where the plows had pushed it off the streets. It would take days, and perhaps weeks, for all of this to melt and disappear. Sara struck a pose in front of a jagged mound that reached up to her shoulder, and, squinting into the sun, had Edie snap her picture for the folks back home. Danny would be madly jealous, but no doubt, sooner or later, his turn would come.

Later, in school, she was one of the first to finish the Navi test, and knew she had done well. When the bell rang for recess, Morah Jacobs asked Edie to step outside to speak with her in the hall. Sara saw Edie's puzzled frown, and watched her trail after the teacher. What had she done this time?

Was there no end to it all? How easy it would be to shrug this off and say, 'Who cares what she's gotten into now; it's no skin off my back!' Why did she always feel pulled in two directions?

Normal life on the one hand, and Edie's tense, complicated existence on the other.

Elisheva Marcus was telling everyone about the upcoming visit of her married brother's family. All the girls had gotten to know him and his wife last year at the annual Chanukah *chagigah* when he had been the guest speaker.

"I wish he'd come and speak again. He was great!" said Irena, a Russian girl who was one of the top students in the class.

"What's the theme this year, does anyone know?" asked Mirel. "Oh, Sara! The *chagigah* is fabulous. Just wait! Y'know what? On the way home this evening I'll sit on the bus with you and tell you all about it."

Sara smiled. If it weren't for her ever-present problem, she could be very happy in this terrific school.

Edie walked in late to the next class but was excused when she handed the Historiah teacher a note. She looked blank, as usual. Sara writhed in her seat and tried to focus on the Middle Ages.

Mirel kept her word. On the bus trip home, without coming up for air, she spouted a steady stream of superlatives, painting a vivid picture of last year's *chagigah* for Sara.

"The whole school participates in the program and all the arrangements. Last year our class was in charge of the decorations — you know, color scheme, tables, centerpieces. It's only three or four weeks away now!"

Sara stared out the window. Her mind shut out the babble and drifted 1600 miles back to Texas. They'd had their very first high school concert for girls and women last Chanukah. The whole affair from A to Z had been set up, directed, and orchestrated by Mrs. Deutch. A trial balloon that really soared!

"What did you have in your school last Chanukah?" Mirel was asking.

"We had a band, some dances, and a skit," she answered, surprised at how low key it all sounded. But then, Mirel would never be able to understand how they'd felt peeking out from behind the curtain when the hall had filled up, until there was standing room only! Who would have believed Mrs. Deutch could pull this off? And the standing ovation at the end! She shook her head and looked at her friend. "It's a lot different out of town," she said. "Hey, I wonder why Morah called Edie out. Any idea?"

"Who knows? Mind you, I think Morah's well aware of the fact that Edie doesn't exactly have a crush on her! I mean, with the way Edie acts in her classes, that's pretty obvious. Still, just clamming up and gazing out of the window as if you're bored silly isn't enough of a reason to — "

The end of the sentence got lost as the bus came to a sudden halt, and everyone got off.

But Sara, really curious by now and waiting impatiently for the right opening to get to the bottom of this, was taken totally by surprise when Edie announced at the supper table: "Morah Jacobs asked me to speak at the Chanukah *chagigah*."

"She did?" Shira was all smiles. "That's great!"

"Is it?" Edie's voice gave nothing away.

"Well, isn't it?" asked the Rebbetzin. "I should think that's quite an honor. Would you please pass the vegetables, Moish?"

"It sure is!" Shira said. "This year, for the first time, they're picking one girl from each class to speak instead of getting a guest speaker. The G.O.'s suggestion, I may add, modestly!" she said, managing to pat herself on the back. "But, of course, it was up to the teachers and Rabbi Solomon to decide who would be chosen."

Ezriel, who had been busy designing his initials in straight lines of peas, now chimed in.

"What are you going to say?"

"Will you please stop pushing your food around, Ezriel, and eat! I want to see a clean plate!" said Mrs. Rudin. "What *is* your topic, Edie? Do you know already?"

"Sort of. Yes!" Edie said, "Each one of us has been asked to discuss one part of the miracle of Chanukah. First the historical aspect, and then how it applies to us today." She speared a piece of salmon and popped it into her mouth, chewing with relish.

Sara couldn't believe what was going on. Edie hardly ever spoke at the dinner table, and never unless she was addressed directly. She ate sparingly and always escaped as quickly as she could. Tonight she was the center of attention, and her appetite was apparently excellent!

"Are you nervous?" asked Yocheved, her face clearly showing how she would feel if this were her assignment.

Sara watched Mr. Rudin as he looked at Edie intently, waiting for her answer.

"Not very," said Edie with a grin. "It's only the girls and the teachers. Right, Shira? No parents!"

"Right! But still, it's about 150 people, give or take a few. You'd better make it interesting!"

"Oh, she will!" said Mr. Rudin. "And I want a tape of her speech, Shira. Make sure they record all four of them. Well, Edie, you'll put us on the map. Your father will be so proud." He wiped his mouth on his napkin and look at his watch. "No dessert for me tonight," he said. "I've got to run. Sorry, Faye — but isn't this nice news?" He made a *brachah acharonah* and rushed out of the room.

"Did she say which part of the *neis* you're to speak about?" Sara asked Edie as they stood at the kitchen counter, scraping the dishes and loading the dish-washer.

"Yeah. The stand of the Maccabim and all that. Fighting for what's right even if you're in the minority. Standing up for Torah whatever the odds." She straightened up and looked searchingly into Sara's eyes. "It's so weird that she'd pick me, no? You don't think she knows anything about — you know what? And why would she give me just that particular piece?"

"That's anyone's guess. But of course, she doesn't know anything. She hasn't the faintest idea! Maybe it's because you are an excellent student, probably the best in the class, and you keep showing her you're tuning out, you're not interested, you couldn't care less, and so she's pulling you in by your hair. She's beaten you in this game of tug-of-war, right? Admit it, Edie! You'll speak, and you'll wow them! You have no choice. And who knows, maybe you'll get a kick out of the whole thing."

Edie scooped up a measure of detergent and started the machine.

"I thought I'd say, 'No, thank you, get someone else.' But you know? I surprised myself. Suddenly I knew I wanted to do it. I didn't even argue with her." She snapped her fingers, "Chick-chock. Just like that!"

"Wait till you tell Rabbi Rudin; it'll make his day. I wonder whether he'll find time to finish our 'conference' this evening. Remember, I also have a plan for you, Just-Edie!"

"Hah!" Edie snorted, rinsed her hands, and dried them on a dish towel. "Everyone's trying to organize me. The story of my life! C'mon, let's go to *shaatnez* town."

Rabbi Rudin was indeed impressed with Edie's news. "If you need any help, please ask," he said. "You say they want about five minutes? Wait till you try reading something aloud for that period of time. That's a lot of words! But I have no doubt you'll find plenty to say!

"Okay, now. Let's try to get back to our other subject. We may be interrupted now and then, but let's give it a try. I assume you've both thought about what we heard a week ago, and that you didn't discuss it with one another."

They nodded, and Edie said, "Yes, to both."

"All right, then; let's begin with you, Edie. Where would you like to go from here? That was the question."

"I want to stay in Montford," Edie blurted out. "That is, even after my father comes home, *b'ezras Hashem*. I mean, the truth is I don't really fit in here either, not the way you do, Sara, anyway; but I feel definitely less pressured, less angry, and if I play it low key, there aren't even any confrontations.

"And I've also come up with what I think is really the main reason I'm fighting all the time at home. It's because no one's looking at Me. Like we said, not all people are alike. And me, maybe I'm less alike than most," she giggled. "But I need to be treated as an individual; I can't just be number four in a row of 11 identical pegs."

"Makes sense," said Rabbi Rudin. "Sara?"

"Well, I was thinking about why *I* wanted to come here, and it boils down to wanting more, wanting more in terms of my own *Yiddishkiet* than I can get in Dalton. But what Edie's saying is, she wants to be here because of a bunch of noes and negatives. I know this may sound way off, but what I'm trying to bring out is, we're both running; I'm running towards, and she's running away from."

Sara wiped her sweating palms on her skirt. She knew exactly what she meant to say, but it was hard to put into clear sentences.

"We both need this place, but for different reasons. Like I said, I'm getting a great deal more here than I could at home. It will take years and years (if ever!) for Dalton to look like Montford. But Edie's coming from Boro Park; she's had all that, and more. The way I see it, she needs to find out for herself how much joy and satisfaction there is in a life of Torah. And not as peas in a pod, but each person in their own, individual way."

"Interesting!" said Rabbi Rudin. "Well, Edie, what d'you — "

The doorbell rang and a lady staggered in with an armload of clothing. She was huffing and puffing with the exertion of lugging the clothes out of the car into the office.

"Wait!" she breathed heavily, and dumped the lot into Sara's waiting arms. "There's more!" And she was gone, only to return with an even bigger load for Edie.

"For our *chasanah*," she explained, wiping her face with a moist towelette pulled from her voluminous purse. "I told my sister I'd take her stuff along with mine. Just hold on a minute and let me check that nothing slipped down on the floor of the car."

While she ran out again, the girls began sorting and listing the particulars. The lady returned and kept up a steady flood of comments about each garment, the wedding, all the unexpected problems that were besetting her in connection with the arrangements, and finally the fervent hope that the entire mountain of clothes would be ready for her the following evening.

Rabbi Rudin was kind but adamant.

"You'll probably have everything back by the end of the week. I hope we don't run into any bad problems, and we'll work on them as quickly as possible, Mrs. Nelken. Now, what have we got here, girls? Let's see; four three-piece men's suits, one man's overcoat — "

The phone rang.

Mrs. Nelken had set off an avalanche of business, and Rabbi Rudin suggested they adjourn their conversation until after closing time.

"I'm willing to stay on a little longer to get this straightened out. Okay with you both?"

An hour or so later, they finally settled back, this time knowing that even if the phone rang, there'd be no need to pick up.

"I had one more thing to say," said Sara quickly. "The necklace. It bothers me. I'm not exactly sure what's the right way to go with it, but I don't think we can just ignore it."

"I won't tell Mrs. Rudin," said Edie. "I couldn't survive that."

"Okay," said Rabbi Rudin. "I feel the same way Sara does about the necklace. Let's not 'bury' it twice! I've gone into it myself and discussed it, without mentioning a name, of course, with my *rav*. You do not have to tell Mrs. Rudin, Edie. She will continue wearing it, and neither she nor the boys, nor anyone else around here, need every know.

"However, you should make every effort to pay for it. Remember, there is no *brachah* in anything derived from stealing — ever! Do you know how much it was?"

"Yes," Edie answered in a low voice. "It was $179.95. I tore the ticket off right in this house."

"Would you know the name of the boutique or the address?" persisted Rabbi Rudin.

"Yes." Edie's voice was now scarcely more than a whisper. "I know the name because Tammy kept saying, 'Geo has great stuff!' " She swung her hair over her shoulder. "*Very* nice stuff! She even told me the store's called 'Geo' as in geography, meaning earth. That's because they import their merchandise from all over the world. Oh, well. I guess I could find the address in any Manhattan phone book, and I'll send in the cash." She sounded resigned.

For a moment no one spoke. Rabbi Rudin tilted his chair backward until it teetered on two legs.

"I'll tell you what," he said from his precarious position. "Why don't I lay out the cash, and then I'll deduct whatever amount you suggest from your weekly salary, until you're paid up. But you'll have to write a note saying that you are an Orthodox Jew and that you took this item from their store. Now you feel that you want to make amends and pay in full. The *rav* said you don't have to sign your name or give any return address.

"As for the rest, I don't have to tell you, Edie, that what you did was very wrong. It needs *teshuvah* and the firm resolve never again to get into that kind of thing."

Edie sat silently, her head bowed. Sara felt awful. Should she have brought up the subject of the necklace? But then, Rabbi Rudin himself had obviously planned to speak about it. She wished she could touch Edie, put her arm around her shoulder, and find the words that would make her snap out of this bent, un-Edie-like pose.

As if in response to her silent wish, Edie sat up straight.

"Okay; thanks a lot! I'll pay it off and I'll write a masterpiece. Rabbi Rudin, I really appreciate your advancing the money, because my cash flow isn't the greatest right now. But — what do you think about my staying here?"

"I'm all for it, if it can be worked out," said Rabbi Rudin. "Of course, you should be home for winter break when your father, all being well, *b'ezras Hashem,* gets back. You should definitely go home for Pesach, but I very much hope you'll be able to finish the school year in Montford, boarding right here, with Sara and the Rudins.

"I would also like your permission to speak to your parents about some of the problems that do exist. Problems that finally led to your 'Tammy fling.' You see, I am a great believer in communication. From what I can tell — and, I may be biased, of course, having only heard your side of the story — there is a great lack in that area in your family. As you said, you are all expected to march in step, and there's very little talking, explaining, or sharing. If there were, there'd be more *simchah* and warmth. See, your father's 100 percent correct in demanding full, unquestioning *kibud av va'eim.* But much of that can come about through a family interacting happily and positively, without constant 'noes'! There are so many ways to achieve the same results, but with gentleness and love. For example, your home need not be run like your father's carpet warehouse, and your mother, too, doesn't seem able to change a situation that must be very hard for her to bear."

Rabbi Rudin got up.

"Think about it, Edie. I'd be glad to call your parents, or wait until they get back from Rochester. Just remember, I've taught for many, many years, and I have dealt with parents all that time. Plus, of course, there's my own *chevrah* at home, and I've learned a thing or two from them also. Believe me, your situation is by no means unique. I've met up with similar problems over and over, and with a little goodwill and some effort on everyone's part, they can usually be greatly improved."

As he reached for his hat and coat, he added, "I'd like to try, if you want me to."

"I do, of course," said Edie. "And anyway, I'll need your help to get their permission to stay here until the summer. That is, if the Rudins will have me."

"Oh, I don't expect we'll have a problem with that. And now, as my brother Moish would say, I really have to run."

Chapter Fifteen

"Where's your mother?" Sara asked Yocheved, who was practicing her recital piece on the piano.

"She had to take Tante Risha to the podiatrist," said Yocheved. "Would you do me a favor?"

"Sure."

"Just sit there in the corner of the couch, close your eyes, and listen. Tell me if it's okay."

"That's not a favor. That's heaven!" said Sara.

They'd gotten to sleep very late last night, and it had been a long, hard day in school. Simmy had given her 20 minutes of extra tutoring in *dikduk* during the lunch hour. Sara was zonked! She slipped off her shoes, folded her legs under her, and rested her head on the back of the armrest, closing her eyes.

"Let's go," she mumbled.

It was a classical piece, and as Sara listened, she realized she'd heard snatches of it during the past few weeks. Wasn't it strange that this timid, shy little 11-year-old played with such confidence! Here's how she can talk without speaking, Sara thought, and express herself without looking straight at anyone. Shira, too, had her music, but for her it was just one more activity, another favorite thing to do.

Soon she'd get her acceptance or rejection from B.M.L. The interview with them had only gone 'kachah- kachah,' as she'd put it, and Sara guessed that this was her way of hiding her hopes and preparing herself for disappointment.

Next year at the Rudins would be very different without Shira, but perhaps Edie would stay. Daddy was getting used to the idea that Sara's heart was set on continuing school here in Montford. And what if she too would end up in Israel after 12th grade? So many years away from home? It didn't bear thinking about!

Yocheved had stopped playing. She got up quietly and walked over to Sara with a questioning look.

"Excellent!" said Sara, sitting up. "Bravo! Really beautiful!"

"I made two mistakes, but you wouldn't notice. I mean, only because you don't play,' she added immediately. "But *Baruch Hashem,* I still have a few more days to practice."

"It was fantastic," said Sara. "Play some more, anything you like, okay? You're really good, you know; even a dummy like me can tell," she added with a grin. "What does Mrs. Ben-Ami say?"

"She's a perfectionist and very strict. The nicest thing she'd say is, 'That was quite good, Yocheved; make it *very* good for next week!' But I love playing duets with her the last few minutes of every lesson. All the scales and exercises are worth it for that!" Her face lit up with pure joy just thinking about it.

"Telephone for Edie," Louisa said, coming from the kitchen. "Where is that girl?"

"I'll get her," said Yocheved. "She's probably in her room."

"She plays beautifully, doesn't she?" said Louisa to Sara, inclining her head in Yocheved's direction. "I could listen to her all day and forget I'm working."

"She's great," said Sara. "When did she start lessons?"

"Seven, I think. She's a wonderful kid. I just sometimes wish I could toughen her up some. Life is full of hard knocks, and that child's soft as butter. Oh, here comes Miss Oppenheim," she added, raising her eyebrows. "Now, there's someone who can take it on the chin!" She laughed and returned to the kitchen.

"Can she?" Sara wondered, lying back and staring at the ceiling. After a few minutes, her eyes began to smart and droop. She realized she'd dozed off when Edie returned.

"So that was your little secret scheme, Sara Hadassa!" she said.

Sara blinked and rubbed her eyes.

"Sorry, didn't mean to wake you up. That was the J.E.P. office, a girl called Reva Something."

Sara nodded sheepishly.

"Why didn't you ask me yourself?"

" 'Cause."

" 'Cause why?"

"Just 'cause. Now let me go back to sleep."

"Don't you want to hear what I said?"

"Tell me," Sara murmured drowsily.

"I said, 'Why do you want to take a chance on a misfit like me?' and she said, 'You came highly recommended, and I'm not worried one bit. How does that grab you, Miss Oppenheim?' "

Sara, eyes still closed, began to hum the catchy melody of Yocheved's Mozart.

" 'You may be in for a shock,' I told her. 'I'm not crazy over kids, you should know.'

" 'You will be,' she said. 'They're a great bunch, and Sara will be around to help you out. It's too many for one leader.' And before I could even say, 'I'll think about it,' she said, 'I'm so glad you can start this week because it's really not fair to Sara — I mean 16 seven-year-olds! So thanks a million. See you there!' And on that happy note she slammed down the receiver. DO YOU HEAR ME, SARA?" Edie yelled.

"You're a doll, Just-Edie, for offering your services. A heart of gold you have, and I never knew it! Believe me, I'm deeply touched. Now, will you please quit it and let me get a nap before supper? PLEASE?"

"Ugh!!" Edie gave a snort and stomped out of the room.

"How did it go, Sara?" asked Mrs. Rudin on Shabbos afternoon when the two of them, alone in the kitchen, were cutting up vegetables for *Shalosh Seudos.*

"Fine," said Sara. "The kids loved Edie; I knew they would."

"I'm thrilled," said Mrs. Rudin. "I think she's really coming out of her shell now, and Uncle Meyer says she'd like to stay on. It's fine with us. We enjoy our boarders, and it's gratifying to know we're making it possible for girls to study here. But it works both ways, you know. I need the peace of mind that goes with having responsible people in the wing near the Rebbetzin. She has a rubber-tipped cane, and if ever, G-d forbid, she should need help at night, she can always bang on your wall. That's a great source of comfort to me, knowing we have two big girls close by." She placed a cherry tomato atop the center of the platter and handed it to Sara to take into the dining room.

"What are we having?" Naftoli, who had just sidled in, reached over and helped himself to half a deviled egg.

"*BRACHAH!*" Mrs. Rudin seemed to have eyes in the back of her head.

"Ezriel punched me in the stomach, and Shaya wants to eat over. Can he, Ma?"

"He's welcome, but only if his mother knows. Let him run over and ask. We'll be sitting down in 10 minutes, so get everyone over here, please. Thank you, dear."

For Shabbos lunch there had been 21 people, about average for this household. But *Shalosh Seudos* was usually a casual affair, mostly for family. When the girls went out to the kitchen to get the ices, Edie asked Shira whether outsiders could be invited for the Chanukah *chagigah.*

"See. I know this girl in Brooklyn, and I'd like to ask her. D'you thing they'd let her come?"

Shira gave this some thought, while Sara clenched and un-clenched her fists.

" Well, the concert's different, of course. It's for everyone; the more the better. The *chagigah* I'm not sure about, but you could ask Morah Jacobs. With you being one of the speakers, she'd probably make an exception. I'm sure your friend could sleep over with us; it goes on till very late, you know. What's her name?"

"Tammy," whispered Sara.

"Tammy," said Edie. "Tammy Weisser."

Morah had apparently given the okay, and Edie made the call from their bedroom on Sunday afternoon. Sara understood that this was a private phone call, and without having to be asked, she had gone next door to have a little chat with the Rebbetzin. She felt very apprehensive about Tammy's coming, but she did not want Edie to know or even suspect her feelings.

Mrs. Rudin's words still rang in her ears. Surely it wasn't just the comfort of knowing they were nearby in case of an emergency, *chas v'shalom;* surely she also expected them to try to be a bit neighborly toward the elderly lady 'on their block.'

She knocked and waited for a response. The humming sound of a tape recorder came through the door.

"Come in!"

"Hi! Am I disturbing you now, Rebbetzin?"

"Not at all. Sit down over there while I shut this off. I like to lis-ten to these *shiurim* while I sew." She was hemming a pair of pants for one of the boys, and several other jobs patiently waited their turn on a nearby chair.

Sara sat on the love seat that faced the Rebbetzin.

"Sit back, relax! Or maybe you'd like a sewing lesson?"

Sara grinned. Why not? "Okay. Good idea! But start me from scratch, please."

"Done!" said the Rebbetzin.

She sent Sara to the wall closet to bring her a large bag full of old, clean rags and some remnants of material. From this, she fished out a square piece of sprigged cotton fabric. Patiently she showed Sara how to backstitch for a hem. It wasn't too complicated, and Sara settled back into her corner, biting her lower lip in concentration.

"When you've hemmed that around, we'll promote you to fixing Yocheved's Shabbos skirt. The hem's halfway down. So tell me some news."

Sara's thread had just knotted up badly, and she was debating whether to tear it off and start over, or to fake it and just continue with what was left.

"Our class is in charge of all the food for the Chanukah *chagigah*. Seems they have more or less the same traditional latkes and doughnuts every year. They make everything in school because of the *kashrus*, you know. Can you think of anything a little more original that we could make?" She had decided to ignore the knot and just continue sewing until the thread gave out. It was more fun than she'd expected.

"Hmm. Why don't you and Edie borrow Mrs. Rudin's Chanukah cookie cutters, or buy a set if they don't permit utensils from home, and bake a few platters of *dreidel*, candle, and *menorah* cookies? I have an old recipe that can't be beat. I'm sure they'd be a big hit."

"Wow! That sounds great!"

There was a slight rap at the door, and here was Edie! Rudely ignoring the Rebbetzin, she turned to Sara.

"She's not coming." Her voice was rough.

"Why not?"

"She's just not. She's not interested. She says I have to make up my mind; it's up to me. Either I stick with her and her crowd, or choose the other way and 'play safe,' as she puts it. That's about the gist of it."

Edie never once looked at the Rebbetzin or acknowledged that this conversation was taking place in her private sitting room.

Sara couldn't bear it.

"Edie's invited an old school friend of hers to our party," she said to the Rebbetzin by way of explanation. "So what did you answer?" She turned her attention back to Edie.

"I told her she sounded like Avraham talking to Lot: 'You go right, I'll go left,' and never the twain shall meet. And she said,

'Exactly!' And then I said, 'You sure?' and her answer was, 'Absolutely! That's *not* my scene, and you know it, Edie!' It was like a fencing match! So then I said, 'Well, for now, I'll choose the RIGHT.' She didn't seem too happy about that, but wished me good luck. What on earth are you sewing there, anyway?" Edie plopped herself down next to Sara and snatched the crumpled scrap of material away from her.

"That's Sara's first sewing lesson," said the Rebbetzin with great dignity, "and from what I have just heard, it seems to me that both of you have been most gainfully occupied during the last half hour!"

Chapter Sixteen

The night before the *chagigah,* Rabbi Rudin told the girls that he had had a long conversation with Edie's father and mother. Mr. Oppenheim was recovering well from his second bout with surgery, and *b'ezras Hashem,* he'd be home the first week in January. He and his wife were counting the days! Rabbi Rudin had then explained the reason for his call, and without going into a detailed recap of the conversation, he had apparently convinced them that it was in Edie's best interest to finish the year in Montford. Of course, she'd be home for winter vacation and Pesach, but she was really doing so nicely here that it would be a shame to change schools at this point.

"I also tried to touch on some of the problems we discussed in the shop, and I believe they understood that there were things that could be improved if everyone communicated a little better. Let's just say it was a beginning. Your father's been through so much, Edie! He's lost a lot of weight, and he's also quite subdued. My feeling is, he's just so happy to be alive; that's all that matters right now. Incidentally, I thought they were really very gracious in the way they responded to me, a complete stranger, mixing into their business!"

"I just don't know what to say, except thanks a million!" said Edie. "You know, now that you've broken the ice, I think I'll write them a special letter. It'll be easier than a conversation on the phone."

They talked a little about Shira's disappointment. The letter from B.M.L. had said that she was on the 'pending' list. The other seminaries to which she'd applied would not respond until January. For now, she was in limbo. Poor Shira! She was pretty devastated. Two of her closest friends had been accepted to B.M.L. and they'd been keeping it a secret, not knowing where she stood. She'd overheard a younger sister of one of the girls tell a friend.

Everyone at home tried their best to say the right things, but although Shira kept assuring them that she'd expected it all along, their hearts ached for her.

"She'll be fine in any seminary, I just know it," Sara said. "But right now it's tough."

"She doesn't feel like going to the *chagigah* tomorrow night, but I don't think she's got a choice. Head of the G.O. and all that," said Edie. "I told her she's got to come give me moral support. But she said she needs more of that than I do."

They had followed up on the Rebbetzin's suggestion, and the 10th graders had baked dozens and dozens of Chanukah sugar cookies that afternoon. It had been great fun, and the results were spectacular. Edie had begged off because she had a splitting headache and because she still had some work to do on her speech.

"Has she read it to you?" Simmy asked Sara.

"Nope. She's keeping it under wraps. She hasn't even gone to Rabbi Rudin for help, and he offered!"

"She's a brain!" said Shaindel. "You wait; this speech is going to be something else!"

The girls were reserving judgment. Ever since Morah had picked Edie to represent them, their attitude had begun to veer from totally negative to — well, maybe, after all?

When Edie walked up to the lectern to speak, she had 102 degrees fever, but no else knew except Sara. It had been building up over the last 24 hours, and at one point in the afternoon she had asked Sara to pinch-hit and read the speech for her. But Sara, although fully aware of the flushed face and unnaturally bright eyes, had refused.

"You'll douse yourself with Tylenol, and Shira will drive you home the minute you're finished," she had said. She was convinced that the Shabbos group, along with this speech, would turn things around for Edie. And just as Edie had to face those kids every Shabbos afternoon in the role of group leader and deal with them, *she* herself should be the one to speak tonight. Something told Sara that in a way, Edie would be speaking to herself, out loud.

Edie surveyed the crowd and waited for silence. Sara noticed that there were no notes, and that Edie emanated a sense of total control. And then, almost in a monotone, she began:

"Imagine you're a girl living with your family in the time of the *Chasmonaim.* For years the Jews have been oppressed, crushed, and humbled by taxes imposed on them by various rulers. Sums that just cannot be raised. And now, under Antiochus, *shmiras hamitzvos* — such as Shabbos, *bris milah,* and Rosh Chodesh — are forbidden — at the risk of death!

"It has become hard to remember what *Yiddishkiet* was like when things were different. Now it's a living nightmare! And so, the unbelievable has come to pass! Many Jews, some of your best friends' families, are happily accepting Hellenism. They enjoy all the luxuries offered by the Greeks. The beautiful, enormous gymnasium very near the *Bais Hamikdash* in Yerushalayim is open to anyone who first sacrifices there, in the Outer Courtyard, to the pagan gods. *Avodah zarah* paves the way to joy and comfort, to a guarantee of safety and wealth.

"And then, supposing your father called a family meeting in

secret and said, 'I'm not as learned as some, but look, there's Mr. So-and-so, a member of the *Kohen Gadol's* family, a respected man, a *chashuv* man, and he's chosen to go over to them. He, and all his cousins and friends. And what about our neighbor, who always had so much wealth that the *aniyim* lined up at his door, and he was there for everyone? Where is he now? Yesterday he invited me to join him for a few hours in the gymnasium. He told me that for one little sacrifice of a pig to their gods, I could have it all. He said I was holding out for nothing, that we were lost, and should face up to reality! "Look," he said, "they've already plundered the *Bais Hamikdash* and stolen our holiest *keilim*. They're sacrificing pigs right in there." He told me to come with him, that my life and the lives of my loved ones were placed in jeopardy because of my stubbornness. But I refused — this time.' "

Edie continued to paint the scene. She had done a lot of research, and those days in history sprang to life as she portrayed the farmers laboriously scratching the words '*Ein li chelek be'Elokei Yisrael*' into the horns of the oxen that pulled their plows.

"Can you imagine driving through Montford with a sticker on your windshield that says 'I have no part in the G-d of Israel'? And that if you refused to put it there, you'd be sentenced to death? Can you imagine having your front door forced from its hinges, your home laid open to vandalism and worse, every shred of your privacy destroyed?"

The girls were riveted to the low, hoarse voice. Edie's presentation wasn't theatrical; she wasn't the type. But Sara thought this low-key style made the story even more stark and terribly believable.

"Then you try to weigh the pros and cons. Your friends have gone both ways; some have joined the Hellenists, and others are clinging with fierce loyalty to the Torah, crying bitterly in secret over the horror that's played out every day in the holiest place on earth. And there are hundreds like yourself and your family who are still wavering.

"And now there's a call by an old man called Matisyahu, who sends out his cry from the little town of Modin, to which he has fled with his five sons and their families: 'YOU, all of you who are on the side of Torah and *mitzvos*, join with me. We will fight to the last breath to restore our *Bais Hamikdash* to its former splendor. Without our Torah and *mitzvos*, we are nothing. *Mi L'Hashem Eilai!'*

"The question is, could we find it in ourselves to give up so much luxury, wealth, honor, acceptance, comfort, and safety — and choose instead thirst and hunger, freezing cold, heat and dirt, fleeing and hiding, sickness and danger, and perhaps even death, to stand up for our beliefs?" She paused for a moment and then continued. "There were, of course, those who did — *Baruch Hashem.* And maybe some of us would have chosen the same.

"The Maccabim stood at the helm of that small army whose banner was not a battle cry, but instead a proclamation of Hashem's greatness. '*Mi Chamocha Ba'eilim Hashem!*' They provided an alternative to those who wavered. This was a positive choice they could make. And tonight, celebrating Chanukah here in Bais Yaakov of Montford, U.S.A., we are the living proof that in the end, with Hashem's help, they prevailed."

There was a moment of silence, followed by a tremendous round of applause. Edie acknowledged the ovation with a lopsided smile and slowly walked back to her place next to Sara.

"Absolutely super!" Sara whispered. "Look at Morah Jacobs! She's beaming at you! It was fantastic! How do you feel?"

"My head's spinning out of control. I bet my temperature's up to 103! Can you ask Shira to drop me off? I know it's not fair to take her away right now, but — " Her voice trailed off to a sigh.

Five minutes later she was gone, and the girls were listening to an 11th-grader speak about *Shemen Zayis.*

Making the right choices, that's what it's all about, Sara thought. Wow! What a powerful speech! You did okay, Just-Edie!

With a delicious feeling of relief, she settled back in her seat and began to enjoy herself.